T0158937

Sheep EATERS

Jill Van Horn

WESTBOW
PRESS®
A DIVISION OF THOMAS NELSON
& ZONDERVAN

Scripture quotations are taken from the Holy Bible, New International Version®, NIV®. Copyright © 1973, 1978, 1984, 2011 by Biblica, Inc.'™ Used by permission of Zondervan. All rights reserved worldwide.

WestBow Press books may be ordered through booksellers or by contacting:

WestBow Press
A Division of Thomas Nelson & Zondervan
1663 Liberty Drive
Bloomington, IN 47403
www.westbowpress.com
1 (866) 928-1240

ISBN: 978-1-5127-7413-9 (sc)
ISBN: 978-1-5127-7414-6 (hc)
ISBN: 978-1-5127-7412-2 (e)

Library of Congress Control Number: 2017901758

Print information available on the last page.

WestBow Press rev. date: 02/06/2017

PROLOGUE

My sheep listen to my voice;
I know them, and they follow me.
—John 10:27 (NIV)

"WHAT ARE YOU IN THE mood for?" Fred asked his younger son, Stan, who was sitting in the backseat of the bus with his brother, Nolan, and sister, Bethany. It was misting outside on this particular day in late November, and the unseasonable heat of the day caused steam to rise from the back-country road as the recent snowstorm seemingly melted away into thin air. The old white tour bus with the partially lit sign above the windshield proclaiming their destination to be "He_ven" bounced down the Tennessee road through the vapors.

"I thought it was my turn to choose, Dad," said Nolan.

Fred knew better than to get involved in this sprouting disagreement and gave Stan a knowing look. Stan caught on and responded, "Pizza!" Nolan, who was obviously satisfied, dropped the issue in a split second. Fred was relieved.

For the most part, the Powers family got along well, even if they were living in close quarters on the family tour bus. They were willing, though, to sacrifice a regular, more traditional life in order to spread the gospel across the country by performing concerts in churches with their band, Heaven Express. It was the patriarch of the family, Fred Powers, who preached in these churches and led people to Jesus with his sermons. Fred had found the key to success in this regard was to add humorous life events into his sermons—pure, simple, no-nonsense humor, even if it involved a few exaggerations of the truth here and there to get his point across. He was in his early fifties and an average man, with average height and looks in every sense of the word. He had wiry brown hair with an occasional pesky silver strand poking through, but he did a good job dyeing those with his store-bought auburn-brown hair dye from Walgreen's. His personality was what set him apart from every other average, middle-aged, fiftyish-year-old male.

His wife, Betty, had fallen in love with him for his sense of humor, and his joke-telling kept her in good spirits. An occasional exaggeration didn't bother her a bit; it was part of the package. She was as average-looking to the women of their fifties as Fred was to his fifty-year-old counterparts. Her smile was stunning, however, in that it seemed to spread a light that let you see right down into her heart. She could make you feel like you were the only person in the room. She truly did love everyone. For some Christians, there was always that one person—sometimes even their own relative—who just seemed like an impossible feat to love, the one who actually made them question their own hearts and repent and repent over not being able (or sometimes even willing) to give that person the time of day. But not with Betty. She found something to love about everyone and focused on that. She was the single reason they picked up so many strangers on their travels, sometimes to the dismay of Fred, who would let thoughts creep into his mind that their safety was a concern. But Fred was glad that Betty loved him the way she did. And Betty felt that Fred's storytelling was a way to handle some of the long days of traveling on the road.

Of the three children, Stan stood head and shoulders above the rest, literally. He was only thirteen, but at five foot nine, he was already taller than his eighteen-year-old brother, Nolan. He had a quirky way about him, receiving the humorous, good-natured personality of his dad as well as the loving side of his mother. He had short brown hair and a young Bill Murray look to him. There was something endearing about him that you just couldn't put your finger on, but after a while, you realized that even at a young age, like his mother, he was able to talk to you like you were the only person that existed. Stan was the most affected by the tall tales his dad told. Sometimes he just wasn't sure what to believe when it came to his father's storytelling. He felt a little strange watching his dad tell people something that wasn't quite true. But he saw how people responded and thought to himself, *It's just another way to win a soul—and perhaps make a friend.*

He would never forget one little story his dad had told him. He still didn't know if it was true exactly, but his dad swore on the Bible that it was. Stan started to think about that story again. He was not sure how many times he had thought of it in the last few years, but he never grew tired of it.

One day, the Powers family pulled into a gas station on the way to a small town in Tennessee. Fred asked, "Does anyone need to use the bathroom?"

"No, Dad," the kids responded in unison.

"Okay, well, I'm going to go use the restroom. I'll be back in a few minutes."

As Fred was walking back to the bathroom, he overheard a conversation between the two employees at the front counter area. He thought he heard his name, so he continued to listen.

"Well, I'll tell you what, Butch. The only way you could get me to go to church next week is if your preacher friend from Washington, Fred Powers himself, walks in and invites me," said Jesse jokingly. He was a large white man with a receding hairline, sitting on a stool just slightly too small for his weight. Anyone listening closely would have been able to hear the stool complaining as it creaked with each move of Jesse's body. He was getting tired of Butch raving about Fred Powers's radio show.

"Okay, Jesse, have it your way. Someday you'll wish you had come with me," said Butch. Fred smiled and walked back to the bathroom.

When he returned a couple of minutes later, he walked up to the gentleman at the counter and said, "Hi, Jesse, you don't know me, but my name is Fred Powers. Your friend Butch here wanted me to invite you to church this weekend. I hope you can make it," Fred smiled and walked out the door, leaving them both with their mouths hanging open. Fred skipped back to the bus, smiling from ear to ear, to tell his family what had just occurred.

"Stan, Stan, did you hear my question?" His sister interrupted his deep thought.

"I'm sorry, Bethany. I must have been daydreaming," he said.

"Well, I was just asking what song you wanted to start with tonight." They were performing at the Higher Power Church in Knoxville, Tennessee.

It was the first time they would be visiting Knoxville. They had been on the road for over five years now, and Stan was thinking about all of the hard work involved in ministry. He knew his dad's philosophy: "The show must go on." *No matter what,* Stan thought. A memory came to mind of his sister, Bethany, who at age twelve had not been feeling well prior to the performance. When they got up to perform, his sister threw up into the microphone during their first song. Bethany kept singing, though, the best she could. Stan remembered thinking that she seemed like a crazy circus monkey that day—she just kept on singing her heart out. He laughed to himself now at how ridiculous that must have seemed to the onlookers, to not take her off the stage.

As much as Stan liked to visit these new churches, he was excited to visit his grandparents as well. It was getting close to the Christmas season, and he was looking forward to going to Olympia to stay with them for a few short weeks to celebrate the holidays. Sometimes it was nice to be in one spot for a while and eat a home-cooked meal. He couldn't wait for Christmas. He loved presents. He didn't get much for himself on the road and always had to share with his siblings. Sometimes he just wanted to have his own stuff. He liked nice clothes and was lucky to be the bigger of the two boys and pass on the clothes he outgrew to his older brother, Nolan, instead of the usual hand-me-downs. *Guess they are "hand-me-ups,"* Stan thought with a laugh. Stan didn't mind traveling, though. He even liked to learn on the road. His mom, Betty, homeschooled Bethany and him—who were only one year apart at thirteen and fourteen years of age, respectively. Fred liked to joke that Stan was in the bottom half of his class because he had a sister.

"I think we should do our original song, 'Arise,'" Stan said. *Try not to throw up into the microphone.* He bit his tongue to stop himself from saying it out loud.

"That sounds like a plan," Bethany said. Their bus pulled into the parking lot of one of the kids' favorite restaurants, Pizza Hut. They proceeded into the restaurant and ordered two large pepperoni pizzas. This wasn't their normal style of eating, as they really tried to eat healthily on the road, but it was a nice treat for them on a performance night. After the meal, Fred and Stan were walking to the restroom to wash their hands when Fred was approached by an older lady with a walking cane.

She moved very slowly toward him, as Stan had already made it into the men's room. She must have been at least eighty, but her eyes seemed to be those of a young woman. They were splashes of a light greenish-blue, like two pools of swirling ocean water on the canvas of a watercolor painting. But more than that, Fred was struck by the translucent skin of her face that seemed to radiate from underneath, a controlled energy enclosed by a skin membrane that almost invited you to touch it just to see if your fingertips would feel a surge of electricity. She seemed frail yet powerful at the same time.

"Hello, Fred. I have a message for you from God." When she spoke, Fred did not expect the high frequency of her voice to penetrate his chest wall the way it did. He couldn't really tell if he was hearing her through his ears, or if the disturbance of the atmosphere and the resulting rapid oscillation of sound waves was transporting the energy of her voice directly into his heart. Fred was frozen for a moment, gasping for breath. If it was any other person, he would have just thought, *Great, a message just for me. Seems like He would just tell me Himself if He wanted.* Due to the presence of this current messenger before him, however, all he could manage to finally say was, "Okay, thank you."

"God is happy with your service. Continue living out God's plan, and you will see how God awards the faithful. You will be like King Solomon," she said and turned to slowly walk away. Fred was stunned into a catatonic state. He had been concerned for a long time about how they were going to be able to afford getting off of the road someday. They didn't have the money to buy a house and hardly any for a down payment. He thought about how he spent most mornings in prayer, before his wife or the kids awoke, speaking with God about their future life.

After what seemed like many minutes, Fred was able to gather his thoughts and get his body to move again. And move he did, as fast as his legs could carry him, into the restroom to grab Stan to have him listen to what the mysterious lady had just spoken to him. As he and Stan came back out, the lady was nowhere to be found.

"Who was it Dad?" Stan asked.

"She was just here a minute ago." It was a little odd, now that he thought about it, that she could have walked away so quickly. She was so frail and walked so slowly. He looked out the front door of the restaurant but did not see her. It was then that he realized that she might have been an angel. Fred was secretly elated at the thought that he may have just spoken with an angel.

"I guess it's too late now," Fred said. Trying to decide if he should tell Stan what he thought. He decided against it for now. *Maybe I'll tell the family later*, he thought. When they got to the church sixty miles down the road, they were greeted by Reverend Will.

"Hello, Powers family!" he shouted from twenty yards away. "Glad you could make it." Stan could make out the shape of a large black man wearing a short-sleeved plaid button-up shirt and khaki pants, walking toward him with a big smile on his face. As he walked up, Will extended his hand to Fred and then to Betty. The three kids stood and smiled at the man. It was obvious that Will had been looking forward to meeting Fred and his family.

"It isn't too often that we get to have a special guest band and speaker all at once. We've been looking forward to this evening for some time now," Will said.

"Thank you, Will, for the warm welcome," said Fred.

"Oh, please call me Willie; that's what everyone calls me."

"Okay, thank you, Willie," said Fred.

"Let me know where to send the helpers to unload the equipment," Willie said.

Fred was grateful for the help. "Great, just send them out here, and we can put them to work," Fred said. After everything was unloaded, the Powerses got ready for their performance. Once they were done, Fred got up to preach. The people of the congregation as a whole were upbeat and smiling, as they had just sung and listened to several good Christian rock songs performed by his family. Fred decided to speak on faith this night, as he usually did. This time he seemed to speak from a renewed faith of his own, and he could feel it well up from inside. He believed people needed to hear the message on faith and have it change their lives—from how they thought, to how they spoke about things, and eventually how they lived out their lives. He spoke for about forty-five minutes before drawing to a close.

"I hope you enjoyed the evening. My family enjoyed spending the evening with you," he said. After the service, a few people came up to him to ask for prayer for a specific issue with which they were dealing. One person in a wheelchair needed prayer for healing of a broken neck, and one person needed a new washing machine. Fred smiled to himself, *Sometimes God works in the small things just to let you know He is still there by your side, ready to help with the big things.* After most of the congregation cleared the sanctuary, he helped with the tear-down process of the band's equipment. A thin tall man in his early thirties, wearing a light brown trench coat and wide-brimmed black hat, walked up to him and tapped him on the shoulder.

"Mr. Powers?" the man said.

"Yes?" Fred turned around and responded with a raised eyebrow, not sure what to expect. The person he saw in front of him, although a young male, reminded him of the elderly lady who had come up to him earlier. He had a "glow" about him, an energy under the skin as well, that almost seemed to draw him closer as if by an unseen force. He felt mesmerized by the words coming from his mouth.

"God is happy with your service. Continue living out God's plan, and you will see how God awards the faithful. You will be like King Solomon."

"Ha … how do you know that?" Fred stammered.

"Because God told me—and He also told me that you were just told the same thing at a restaurant about sixty miles back. I'm just delivering it a second time, so you know it's really God speaking." Then he turned and walked out. Fred was frozen for what seemed like a few minutes before his mind began to function again. *Just like that,* Fred thought, *God just sent a second messenger to me! Wow! Boy, I can't wait to tell Betty and the kids.*

After they had loaded up the bus and were on the road, Fred finally told the kids the story of the two angels, or prophets from God. He wasn't quite sure who they were, but it really didn't matter one way or the other. He did feel the strong presence of God when both of them were talking to him. Stan especially liked the prophecies told by his father. At the time, Fred could not know how much they would impact Stan's thoughts. After Stan went to bed that night, he dreamed of a brand new red Ferrari for the family and a beautiful new Martin guitar for himself.

The thief comes only to steal and kill and destroy …
—John 10:10

At the very hour that Stan went to sleep, there was a meeting taking place. The location of this meeting was not anywhere on the earth, as most would assume, but rather in a dark dwelling place outside of earthly dimensions. It was in a boundless realm, the location of which was known only by the supernaturally wicked spirits of Lucifer's family and, of course, God Almighty. The atmosphere was penetrated by a sulfuric odor, and a fiery red fog loomed in the space, which served to form thick walls around the group within. The evil comrades of the 33rd Battalion of the Northwestern United States, more commonly referred to by the human race as angels of darkness, or simply, demons, were having their weekly Madness and Mayhem meeting. And as usual, they were yelling over each other. There were over two hundred in attendance and the head demon, Ashkran, was becoming enraged at the lack of decorum.

"I want order, and I want it now!" Ashkran roared from the front of the room. As soon as the words came out of Ashkran's mouth, the room grew silent. He was one of the original leaders of the demon world. Lucifer himself had appointed him as chief commander over the others. Ashkran looked the part of a leader—an intimidating one. He was over fifteen feet tall and had long black hair that went to his midback and covered an opening from which a thick black webbing could be cast. It was a weapon he liked to use to trap his prey. His greenish-yellow reptilian face was triangular, with a twelve-inch-long forked tongue that abruptly protruded from his mouth at the end of his sentences and wiped both sides of his face as if to clean it. His two major eyes were black with red pinpoint pupils and stretched across the upper third of his face. His two minor eyes were on the back of his head and were smaller and transparent. They allowed him to see 360 degrees at all times. He had no discrete limbs, and the core of his body was a thick sinewy stump that was able to soften and separate into as many limbs as necessary when he needed them. He glided along the floor without any feet but rather with a large tentacle that slithered back and forth, propelling him.

All demons had similar characteristics, but they ranged in height. Some of the less fortunate demons were only two feet tall. As they gained more experience, they were awarded height, up to three inches at a time, for their combat victories. As an unspoken goal, all demons wanted to be as tall or taller than Ashkran, as height was a highly coveted trait. While most of the demon underlings had specific gifts of the anti-spirit, Ashkran possessed all of them in abundance. He was most well-known for his lack of restraint and tendency toward warring with any being who would question his power. He displayed that character trait quite often recently. There seemed to be a growing movement for plots on earth to cause destruction, and Ashkran was becoming jealous of some of the other less important demons for their effective and creative blows to God's children, although he would never admit it.

After what seemed like many minutes, a voice was heard from the back of the room.

"I would like to make a request," declared the eleven-foot-tall demon Wink, most well-known for his ultra-deceitful schemes. "I put in my request last week for the opportunity to attack the child of God, Stan Powers, of the Powers family of Olympia, Washington. He apparently is at a critical fork in the road, so to speak as to a decision he has to make to serve God or mammon. He has the correct personality profile and measured intelligence to be a useful instrument for our purposes. There is no limit to how many souls he could win for us. His potential should not be underestimated." After pausing for dramatic effect, Wink continued. "My surveillance team reported to me tonight that his father, Fred, was recently visited by the angel Dunamis, who humanized himself not just once but on two occasions to speak directly with him."

At the sound of that name, gasps were heard from around the room. No demons in their right minds would ever underestimate Dunamis or anything in which he was involved. There was obviously a significant reason for his two visits. The demons could only guess as to what that significance was. However, it was vitally important that they not be caught off guard.

"I'd like to humbly request, for a second time, the permission to conduct a prolonged, unrelenting attack on Stan's mind, will, and emotions … at least for the next few years, give or take." Wink hung his head in mock reverence to Ashkran, mostly to hide the sly smile forming at the corner of his reptilian mouth. The other demons snorted with delight at the choice of his words, as if humility was possible for Wink.

"Silence!" Ashkran hissed. "I already had an appointment to discuss your request with his majesty this morning. He has decided to grant your request. However, I would like to remind you that I pride myself in choosing the right demon to carry out any attack on a child of God, and this mission is especially important if it involves Dunamis. I will be watching you closely, and I will also be assigning to your team two additional comrades, Asm and Chaos. As you know, Asm has been highly decorated for his unrestraint, second only to me. And Chaos is especially full of evil and malice."

Wink thought about his new team members and began to smile. His plans were starting to come together. He began to visualize himself as one of the new leaders of the demon world; and in the earthly world, Stan's soul hung in the balance.

Part
ONE

CHAPTER 1

"HOW WOULD YOU LIKE TO learn to trade FOREX, Dr. Carroll? It's a great way to make money," said Tim, a pharmaceutical representative for Eli Lilly. That sounded good to Laura, she was at her wit's end with her career. She had been in private family practice for ten years now, and it was starting to wear her down, especially with the health care reform and new regulations. She didn't know about other physicians, but she was still doing well, in spite of it all. Still, she couldn't help but think about what things would be like if she had taken another path in college and entered another field entirely. She often wondered what her purpose really was. She stood five foot three, and she was in her early thirties. When she first started her practice, she had braces, which caused some of her patients to comment that their doctor looked like she was twelve years old. She smiled her contagious smile now as she thought of that and wished they still made those kinds of comments, but she was getting older now, and she didn't feel like a young lady anymore. In her mind, it seemed the ten years in practice had caused her to age from the stress. In actuality, she still looked younger than some with the same biological age. She tried to stay fit by exercising and eating right when she could. Her philosophy was simple: she couldn't tell her patients to exercise and eat healthful food if she wasn't able to do it herself. She was originally from the East Coast and had gone to medical school in Texas. She liked living in California, but she always had a desire to move back to Texas or the East.

"Well, I like the idea, Tim but I don't know the first thing about FOREX—is it hard to do?" she asked. She knew that FOREX was foreign currency trading, but that was the extent of her knowledge.

"I'm still learning as well, but I'm slowly catching on," said Tim. He had been working on it for about three months and was still trying to practice patience with it.

"Are you making any money yet?" Laura asked.

"Not really. I have a practice account, so the money isn't real. But I turned two thousand virtual dollars into ten thousand dollars in one month!" Timothy wasn't sure how that translated into real money, but he had a feeling that it might change things once he started trading real money. Stan Powers had taught him that the psychology of trading changes once real money is on the line.

"That sounds promising. How did you learn to trade?" she asked.

"PowersFx," said Tim. "It's taught by Stan Powers. He grew up as a minister's son and spent most of his early years traveling in a worship band called Heaven Express. His dad, Fred, still travels as an evangelist and motivational speaker. He's written a few books about faith as well."

Laura thought for a minute about that. She liked the idea of learning from a Christian businessman with an ethical background. In fact, the more she thought about it, the more she liked the idea. "Well, if I were interested, how would I get started?" she asked.

"Just pop onto the website tonight at 11:45 p.m. That's when the webinar starts—since we trade the London market, Stan likes to be online fifteen minutes before the London market opens. He also gives you a two-week free-trial period to see if trading is for you. He basically trades the euro, the European currency, and sometimes the AUD, the Australian dollar, and GBP, the British pound. He does this thing called the 'Birth of a Million,' where he turns two thousand dollars into one million dollars in one year. He's done it three years in a row, each year getting to it quicker and quicker."

"Wow, that sound almost too good to be true," she said.

"I know, but he has a lot of other traders with him in the room, so I know he is the real deal," Tim said.

"Okay, thanks for the information. I'll think about it, Tim." That night Laura spoke with her husband, Ryan, about Tim's suggestion. Laura and Ryan had been married almost ten years, the exact length of her career. Laura first saw Ryan at church after being on call during her residency. She had been barely alive as she sat there, after a long, *long* night of seemingly endless admissions in the Emergency Department, culminating in the

4:00 a.m. delivery of a baby girl. Ryan was standing a few rows in front of her, and when the pastor told everyone to stand and greet a neighbor, he turned three-quarters of the way around, and she saw his cute smile and right dimple. He was also very tan and muscular and was wearing a bright white T-shirt. She perked up quickly, and her mind started to wonder who this person was. *Does he live in this city? Surely, he must be taken … but he is alone.* She tried to convince herself of the possibility that he was single. She left church that day wondering if she'd ever see him again. *That's funny,* she thought. *I can't remember the pastor's message.*

As God's perfect timing would have it, she saw him again about five months later as she was leaving church and walking toward her car. She felt her heart skip a beat in her chest. As she got into her car, she wondered if she would ever meet him. She drove to Starbucks after church that day, and as she was walking out, the sun was shining brilliantly causing her blonde highlights to glimmer. The sun almost blinded her grayish blue eyes, and as she involuntarily squinted, she had to do a double take to make sure she was really seeing who was in front of her. There he was, that very same gorgeous guy. In the sunshine, his brown skin seemed to glow. She surprised herself by making the first move, asking him if he had just been at church. Time seemed to stop for a moment, as did Laura's breathing. Ryan slowly pulled his sunglasses to the bridge of his nose to reveal his light blue eyes. "Yes. Were you there?"

It only took three months for them to get married, after that providential meeting, and Laura felt that Ryan was the best thing that had ever happened to her. She hadn't realized that she could actually love someone the way she loved Ryan. Her own upbringing didn't really reflect that kind of love, and Ryan had opened her eyes to a better way to live and love. He had a deep love for God, which helped him love her and others.

"I think that sounds like something worth looking into," said Ryan after Laura told him about the conversation with Tim she had had earlier that day. He knew how much Laura wanted to get out of that office. He got to hear about the day's events after work on a regular basis. He didn't know how she could take it much longer. Every day there was a new reason for Laura to want to quit, but she didn't necessarily want to start over in a new career either. It had been a lot of work to get her practice built up to where it was, and the thought of starting over with a new career was too much to think about.

Ryan, on the other hand, was quite happy with his tree service. He loved to climb tall trees and piece them out, limb by limb. Of course, it was very dangerous running the chainsaws and operating the heavy equipment, not to mention the heights he would climb, all by using his rope, harness, a pair of climbing boots, and spurs. Even with all of the inherent dangers, he only had to be stitched up once by his wife. At that time, he had been trying to do an undercut on a large limb fifty feet up in the tree, and the chainsaw reared back at him and cut his forearm. The customer had driven him to Laura's office. "It missed the tendons by less than a millimeter," his wife had said. After putting in twenty-two stitches, he was as good as new. And he never made that mistake again.

"Okay, I guess I'll get on the website and check it out," she said. In the back of her mind she was hoping it wouldn't make her too tired if she stayed up late for a webinar and then went to work the next day. She figured it was worth a try.

After dinner that night, Laura got on the computer and typed Powersfx. com into the address bar; it brought up Stan Powers's website. A video of Stan in a nice dark suit started to play as Laura watched.

"Hello, everyone. I'm Stan Powers of PowersFx. Do you want to control your trading future? Do you want to improve your quality of life? We would love for you to join us on our journey of navigating the markets. We have all of the tools you need to start trading. We will show you how to use our custom charts to make a good trade. Every night I put out my numbers for trading the euro, AUD, and GBP. If you want to become a full-time trader this year, we will show you how to make this work for your life. We will show you how to enter the 'zone' and trade with as little effort emotionally as possible, while maximizing profits. We will teach you how to put goals into your life. We will talk about attitude and knowledge of the markets as well. What kind of trader are you? That will dictate how you trade. If you are a man or woman with a nine-to-five job, then maybe you should learn how to get dressed and walk into your office and trade. If you are a casual trader, then you should expect casual results. We will show you how your personality will dictate your style of trading. When you are ready, you can try to do the Birth of a Million. That is where I take two thousand dollars and turn it into one million dollars each year. All you need is twenty pips per day. I challenge you to take advantage of what we have to offer. You'll be glad you did. You can sign up for our free two-week trial today and be trading with us tonight. All you have to do is download the free Accucharts on our site, and you are ready to go. Once you sign up, you have access to all of my archived video lessons and custom trading charts. I'll see you in the trading room."

The video ended, and Laura was struck by Stan's stature and the way he carried himself. *Wow, he seems bigger than life and so full of energy*, she immediately thought. She was actually surprised by her own surprise! Laura laughed to herself and started to download the Accucharts on to her computer and started the first of many video lessons. She wanted to be ready to go tonight when she got on the live webinar. *First, though*, she thought, *I have to learn what a pip is.*

When they went to bed that night at 9:30 p.m., Laura set her alarm for 11:40 p.m. so she could get up before the webinar started and sign in. When the alarm went off, she got up, trying not to wake Ryan, and took her laptop into the living room. She wore a headset so the sound of the webinar wouldn't disturb her husband.

She signed on to the webinar and waited for it to begin. At exactly 11:45 p.m. she saw the charts open up and heard a familiar voice from earlier that night.

"Hello. everyone. Welcome to the trade room," Stan said. "I see we have a few new traders signed on tonight. To the right of the screen you can see where you can type questions, and I'll try to answer them." Laura saw a lot of people typing in their various salutations to Stan. *This is going to be fun*, she thought.

"Okay, everyone, we have about ten minutes before the market opens. As you can see, there is a Kelpie forming on the ten-minute chart. For those of you who don't know, the Kelpie is my bread-and-butter trade. I'm going to wait a few minutes after the market opens. It's never a good idea to get into a trade right when the market opens. If you are already in a short term trade, you might consider closing it out now. Okay, it looks like we have a report coming out in one hour that might be favorable for the euro. It's an orange report. The orange reports don't move the markets to as great a degree as the red reports. It's always important to see if a report is coming out before making a trade. Let's take a look in the meantime at some of my longer-term charts. The two-hundred-day average chart here is showing a strong trend right now. But the fifty-day average is crossing it here." Stan pointed to one of his custom charts and explained what he was looking at. Laura wasn't quite sure what to make of the charts and had a lot to learn. She was looking at candlestick patterns and all sorts of things she didn't even know existed until tonight. She made a promise to herself to study all of the tutorials by the week's end.

"What did one casket say to the other casket?" Stan asked. He waited for a few seconds and said "Is that you, Coffin?" Laura laughed at the wordplay on 'coughin'." Stan continued to tell stories about the day's events and his thoughts on the market. He joked and laughed with those in the room with him. Laura was starting to get tired. At midnight when the report came out, the euro as compared to the US dollar took a quick spike up and then back down. Stan said it was time to enter the Kelpie trade, and he was going to sell the euro, but Laura wasn't sure how much longer she could stay up. She decided to wait until she reviewed the lessons before making a trade. Even though it was a virtual account, she still wanted to do things right. After a few more minutes of watching the charts, Laura turned off the computer and went to bed. She was excited to get back for tomorrow night's webinar.

CHAPTER 2

THE NEXT EVENING AFTER WORK, Laura ate a quick dinner and went to the bedroom to sit at her desk to learn more about the FOREX market. Tim had mentioned learning the basics of FOREX on a website called Babypips.com. She decided to check it out. Once she got on the website she saw the "School of Pipsology," where they had preschool through graduate school courses on FOREX trading. It was a free website. She started reading about the major currencies such as the USD (US dollar), EUR (euro), JPY (yen), GBP (British pound), CAD (Canadian dollar), and so on. She then read about pips and lot sizes, as well as moving averages, pivot points, and breakouts. As far as she could tell, a pip was a percentage of and the smallest increment in size one could trade with and was a different monetary value, depending on the amount of money you had in your account. She then started reading about candlesticks. The Japanese candlesticks were the main indicator Stan used for trading and the candle formation itself, which was a shaded vertical bar with a thin line extending from its top and bottom, showed the high, low, opening, and closing prices for a certain time period. They could be on a one-minute chart, five-minute chart, or up to a one hour, four hour, or daily chart. On each chart the candlestick represented that chart's time frame. She found the Fibonacci retracements and extensions of the third-grade level to be especially interesting. Fibonacci numbers were based on certain ratios that seemed to be key levels in trading any of the currency pairs. The ratios for Fibonacci were found everywhere in nature, down to the ratio of the length of the bones of your finger to the entire hand, and then from the hand to the forearm, and then the entire arm. These key ratios gave numbers that were used in FOREX to analyze trades. Due to human nature and emotion, over the years—because every trader knew the numbers and used them in their analyses—Fibonacci numbers consistently became areas where the prices of a currency pair would either go to and rebound or break through to the next level. One thing was for sure: they were key areas to watch in any time frame, according to the School of Pipsology.

Laura decided after two hours of studying that it was time to take a break. She had, after all, made it to the fifth grade in only two hours. *Maybe I can graduate by the weekend*, she thought and laughed out loud.

In Olympia, Washington, Stan was preparing his numbers for the night's webinar. Around nine o'clock, the people started to file in. He was used to having a big crowd at his house every night. His wife, Debbie, didn't mind. She was used to having people around. She was a homemaker who enjoyed entertaining. She had a cappuccino machine set up in the kitchen, with soda and snacks as well. Debbie was in her early fifties. She had a pearlike figure and liked to wear bright, colorful loose blouses to take the attention off of her body shape. Debbie felt a little insecure about her size and was currently trying a new diet; one without sugar, and it included the use of a hormone called HCG, Human Chorionic Gonadotropin. It was working well for her as she was able to lose twenty pounds in one month. When Debbie got tired, she just went to sleep in the other room with the family dog, Mocha, a brown toy Chihuahua. Usually, Mocha sat at Stan's feet while he traded, and everyone who came to visit wanted to pet her. Mocha wore a rhinestone-studded pink collar and had her own doggie bed under the desk where Stan traded.

Stan's trading friends from Seattle came to visit and trade several nights a week. Also, his local friends and his best friend and golfing buddy, Paul, who was a real estate agent, came most nights during the week. Paul was sixty-six years old and was semi-retired. He had a lovely wife and three grown children, with three grandchildren. His hope was to retire in one year after successfully pulling off the Birth of a Million that Stan was teaching him. He was still working diligently to realize his goal. Paul was a big help to the new traders. He tried to help the visitors who periodically came from afar to learn how to trade with Stan in person. He showed them some of the custom trades that Stan didn't teach to everyone and some of the other trading systems they were testing.

Stan's monitor setup was impressive. His study was devoted to trading and contained over eight monitors, all mounted to the wall. In the center, he had a live feed of Bloomberg TV. His study was paneled in dark wood and had two built-in cushioned benches, one on each side of the room, for visitors to sit and trade at their laptops. At 11:40, Stan put on his headset to get ready for the live webinar. Paul was helping a visitor named Pam with her charts.

At exactly 11:45 p.m., Stan said, "Welcome, everyone. Tonight we have Pippin' Pam with us, visiting from Colorado. She's been making pips every night with us." Stan pulled up his custom charts. "If you look at my charts here, we got into this trade here last night for forty pips, and then I got into this one earlier today for another thirty. I see Eric got into that one as well. Good job, Eric!" Stan exclaimed as he read through some of the comments. "I put out the numbers tonight, but I'm not sure how much movement we will see, with Friday around the corner. Of course, next week is 'Crazy Friday,' with the red reports coming out for the non-farm payroll (NFP) employment numbers," Stan said. "Let's look at the trend. The EURUSD is in a downtrend and has been for the past six months. I only sell the EURUSD. Call it country pride. I just believe the USD will only go up. That's not to say I don't do occasional scalping, where I will buy the EUR, but that's only short term." Someone asked Stan if he thought he should close out of his trade since he were in a "buy" trade on the EURUSD, and was in the hole two hundred pips. Then Stan asked what percent of the account was in the hole. The person said 25 percent.

"I have the 20 percent rule," Stan said. "Once it's in the hole 20 percent, I would close it out. But you may want to wait for the NFP next week, since those numbers were predicted to be bad for the US and may make the EURUSD climb. I don't usually trade with a stop loss. The 20 percent rule is my stop loss. I enter trades and cost average. I only want to trade 0.5 to 2 percent of my account at a time." The person who was two hundred pips in the hole typed that he was going to hang on for a while longer to see what happened.

It was late February, and Stan said his wife's birthday was coming up. He said, "I'm not sayin' what I'm getting her, but it starts with a 'four' and it ends with an 'arri.'"

I get it, Laura thought. *A Ferrari. That's pretty awesome.* Laura was listening intently to Stan's teaching, and she felt like she was really starting to understand FOREX. She couldn't wait to start real trading. She decided she would trade real money when the NFP number came out next week. *Just a very small lot size, like 0.1 percent of my account*, she thought.

Stan began telling everyone that his two sons, Jason and Jack, had gone around the neighborhood the week before with some buddies from high school and had traded items to get something a little nicer than the item they had before, with the goal of getting something worth a lot more than the original item. When they came to Stan, he had given them a crystal vase in exchange for a golf club. He said they had finally ended up with a 1995 Honda Accord. They then donated the car to their church. Laura liked listening to Stan; he made the trading sessions fun. He really seemed to know the markets well and was able to also joke and tell stories. It seemed like everyone loved trading with Stan.

"Okay, everyone. I'm heading to the yacht for the weekend in Puget Sound. It's beautiful this time of year. Trade safe!" Stan warned.

"Trade safe? Isn't that an oxymoron?" Someone typed.

In the morning, Laura decided it was a good time to finish her lessons in the School of Pipsology. She looked at Stan's website and listened to some of his archived webinars and lessons as well. She was a firm believer in immersion learning. She decided, after looking at Stan's pip calculator, to play around with that for a while. She couldn't help but notice how quickly the money grew—exponentially, when only trading and making 1–2 percent per day profit. She started to multiply the earnings over the month and realized that at that rate, she would be able to close her practice and start trading full time in a matter of months, if all went well. She thought, *If I start with two thousand dollars and start trading and making even just 1 percent a day I will have over a million dollars in less than eighteen months. At that point, I'd be making ten thousand dollars a day!* The thought of that caused her to explore Stan's website for more information that would help her learn how to profit in the world of FOREX. She saw that Stan had a section called "Recommended Reading." She then noticed that his father's books were listed. Most of them had to do with faith and goal-setting. She decided it would be a good idea to check those out. As she was writing down the names of his books, she remembered something she had heard on the television just the day before. She was flipping through the channels and came across a television evangelist. His name was Michael Patterson.

He had said that God was telling someone watching his TV program to believe for a miracle. Also, God wanted to bless us with hidden treasure and that all we needed was favor with one person for our desires and dreams to come to pass. He asked the TV audience to plant a seed of any dollar amount in order to reap a harvest. Laura had thought about it at the time but wasn't sure if she should do it. She had heard many times of what some people called "prosperity preachers," accusing them of wanting your money. But Dr. Patterson said that we were supposed to expect God to bless us—like a farmer who plants a crop with the expectation of a harvest. And thinking about it again now, Laura thought that maybe God was trying to tell her something, that perhaps this was a new chapter for her life.

Laura and Ryan sat down that night to discuss their future and their goals. They wanted to write their goals down on paper. Laura couldn't help but hope that she would be a great trader in the next year or two and would be able to set her own hours. They wanted to travel and help people. Laura wasn't sure what the future held for them, but she was hoping to find out soon.

CHAPTER *3*

TWO MONTHS AFTER STARTING TO trade real money, with Stan's counsel, Laura realized how hard the psychology of trading was. She had read one of the books Stan recommended on his website, called *Trading in the Zone* by Mark Douglas. It was one of Stan's favorites. It was mainly about controlling emotions and learning to follow your own "rules," so to speak, in trading your account. She was having a hard time controlling her emotions. One night she got into a sell trade on the EURUSD, only to decide to exit when it started to go fifty pips against her. A report was coming out that could make it spike one way or the other, and she didn't want it to go against her. She knew she shouldn't have been in the trade to begin with since the setup wasn't quite right, but she had talked herself into it. She broke two of her rules: don't enter a trade right before a report comes out, and don't enter more than 2 percent of your account at one time. She decided to close the trade and lose 20 percent of her account. It was self-punishment for making such a foolish trade.

As she pushed the button to close her trade, it was as if the very push of her button had caused the currency pair to turn around and head into the other direction, the one she had wanted. Laura pounded her fists on the coffee table in the living room. It was 1:00 a.m., and she was tired and upset. She wanted to just throw the computer across the room. *This is not the way it's supposed to go*, she thought. She saw other people typing in to Stan that they had made forty pips—or more—on the report. That just added to her frustration. She decided it was time to visit Stan, if he would agree to it. *There has to be a reason why I just can't get the hang of it*, she thought.

She typed in a question to Stan. "Hi. Stan. I was wondering if I could come visit? I live in California." After a few minutes, she heard Stan say,

"Hey, Laura, I'm sure that could be arranged. Just give me a call later today." He typed his phone number to her. Laura was getting a little nervous now, but she was very excited to have the opportunity to visit Stan and see how he traded in person.

When she woke up later that morning and got ready for work, she decided to call Stan on her way to the office. Stan picked up on the third ring.

"Hi, Stan, this is Laura Carroll," she said.

"Oh, hi, Laura. How are you?" Stan replied.

"I'm doing well, but I'm just having some trouble with following my trading rules and making pips. I wanted to see when a good time might be to fly to visit with you and trade in person. I know it's better if I come during the week for the best trading days," she said.

"How about two Mondays from now? I've got someone else coming in then as well, and you both can learn together."

"Okay," Laura replied with excitement in her voice.

"Just send me your travel itinerary, and I'll pick you up at the airport. You can stay with us or at the hotel down the road. If you mention my name, the hotel will give you a discount."

With the time frame that they were going to be trading, Laura thought it best to stay with the Powers family, and she told him so, adding, "I really appreciate the offer."

"Okay, Laura. You are welcome. I'll see you soon."

Laura made a call to her friend Tim, who had gotten her started on the FOREX trading path with Stan. "Hi, Tim, how is trading going?" she asked.

"Oh, hi, Laura. I decided not to trade for a while. I took a pretty big hit on last Friday's unemployment numbers. I'm starting to think I'm not cut out for trading. How's it going with you?" "Um … I guess okay. I'm actually going to visit Stan to see what I can learn from him in person."

"That sounds good. I'm happy for you! Maybe someday you can help me—if I decide to try again," Tim said halfheartedly.

"You never know, Tim," she said as her typical beaming smile began to emerge. "You just never know."

The following two weeks went by slowly for Laura. She tried to keep trading her account by using her rules but was still watching her account balance dwindle. She knew, though, that once she saw Stan and watched him trade, she would improve her own trading. She just felt like the environment of his trading room, along with the other traders, would give her a better sense of what trades to take and how to better analyze the trades. She was tired of hearing how many pips Stan made each previous night on his numbers, while she missed out. She either had to stay up longer and get even less sleep (which didn't sound very exciting to her) or figure out a better trading system. She hoped this trip would pay off for her; in fact, she was counting on it.

She packed her bags that morning and got ready to fly to Olympia, Washington. Ryan drove her to the Chico airport in record time. They had avoided the traffic by getting Laura an afternoon flight on Monday. She was going to stay for Tuesday and Wednesday, since she was told that was when the volume of trading was the highest. It was the second week of May and it just happened to be her birthday that Thursday. She was excited to go on her trip, although she would miss Ryan and her pets. She had a schipperke, a border collie, and four cats at home. It was a lot of work, but Laura loved animals and didn't mind it at all. She started thinking of how nice it would be to return to celebrate her birthday with Ryan—not to mention that she would have the skills to start being a proficient trader and start on the road to their new future. Ryan said a prayer of protection for Laura, and she went into the airport to check in for her flight.

When they landed in Olympia, Laura went straight to the front door of the small airport. She looked around for Stan, but she didn't see him. She wasn't sure what kind of car he drove, and he didn't know what she looked like. She called his cell phone number, and he answered on the first ring.

"Hello, Stan. I'm here. I don't see you. Are you here?"

"Oh, I wasn't exactly sure what time you were arriving. I'm on my way now. We were just headed over to my sister's house for dinner. Would you like to join us?"

"Sure!" *I don't really have much choice since I didn't rent a car,* she thought. But she was excited to meet the rest of the family. *It's not every day that you meet someone who has millions of dollars and he takes you to meet his family and have dinner.* Laura didn't know what to expect.

"What kind of car should I be looking for?"

"A white Lexus SUV," he responded. "I'll be there in five minutes!"

Sure enough, in about five minutes, Stan pulled up to where Laura was sitting on the bench out front. When he got out of the car, she noticed how tall he was. *He must be at least six foot five*, she thought.

"Hi, Stan. I'm Laura. It's nice to finally meet you in person."

"Hi, Laura. Did you have a safe trip?" He gave her a one-arm hug, took her bags, and put them in the back of his SUV.

"Oh yes, it was fine, just a small delay in Seattle, but everything was smooth."

"Are you ready to eat some dinner at my sister's house? They only live about ten minutes away."

Stan's wife and boys had driven separately and were already at his sister's house. They were used to having visitors from all over the United States come to visit.

"I can't wait!" she said as she got into the Lexus.

They pulled up to his sister, Bethany's, house, and Laura noticed how normal it was. It was nothing fancy. In fact, it was on the smaller side. The Powerses all lived in close proximity to each other. His brother, Nolan, and his wife lived down the street from Bethany. Laura was introduced to Stan's brother, father, and then his wife, Debbie. Laura noted that she had beautiful long dark red hair with bangs that fell just over the top rim of her gemstone-rimmed reading glasses, *or were they real diamonds?* Laura thought as she complimented Debbie on her hairstyle. Debbie was wearing a colorful floral blouse as well as an expensive looking diamond necklace and earring set. She was holding their dog, Mocha, in her lap. There were teenagers in the adjacent room playing the board game Risk.

They had a nice dinner of salad, baked beans, and barbeque from a slow cooker. It was served family-style. Laura noticed that Stan and Debbie didn't eat very much and thought, *Maybe they had already eaten?* Laura felt at home. She was always a little reserved in new places, so she didn't really get the opportunity to talk with Stan's father, Fred, who was deep in conversation with one of the other guests. From watching his demeanor, though, he seemed to be a jovial, animated man. She did speak with Nolan, Stan's older brother. Nolan was also a trader and occasionally taught some of the FOREX classes for beginners online for Stan. Nolan told Laura about a funny trading story when he first started trading.

"I was in a trade, and I decided to take a quick shower. Little did I know a report was about to come out. After my shower, I came back to the computer, and my account had margined out. Needless to say, I was overleveraged! That was a three-thousand-dollar shower that I will never forget," he said, bellowing loudly.

"Wow, I guess I don't feel so bad now," Laura said. She was definitely starting to realize that everyone had a learning curve when it came to FOREX—with perhaps the exception of Stan.

After dinner, Stan took Laura in his car, and Debbie drove the other car home. Stan took Laura on a quick tour of Olympia and around his neighborhood, which was in a nicer area of town at a higher elevation, with a view overlooking the rest of the city. Stan talked about how he first became a trader. He told Laura a story of how he had started to notice that he could see things on the charts that his mentor did not see. One day his mentor called some other experienced traders into the room, and they commented that Stan had knowledge that usually only an experienced trader would have after years of trading. It was at that point that Stan said he knew he was meant to be a trader and that he had a gift. He told Laura about his foundation called Heaven Sent, which helped people across the world by supplying clean drinking water. He said his photographic memory helped him remember trades from five or ten years ago that had the same setup in the past and helped him to recognize good trades.

"It's almost like I can turn on a faucet and have as much money as I want. I have to stop sometimes to leave some for someone else. Remember that those candlesticks we trade represent people. When someone makes money, someone else has to lose," Stan said. Laura knew what that was like. "How is your trading going, Laura?"

"Not so good, Stan, as you probably have figured out by my visit here in the first place," she said. She told him about some of the difficulties she was having with trading his numbers.

"Well, tonight you will have a front-row seat. In the meantime, though, I do have a robot fund I trade that brings in a consistent 4 percent a month. I have two lawyers who watch over it. For the most part, it's automated, but they make sure the computer doesn't have any glitches. You always have the option to invest some money into that while you are learning, only because you are now a part of the 'inner circle.'" As he said that he crossed his second and third fingers in a sign of camaraderie and gave her a knowing look, as if he knew how much she was struggling. Laura didn't think that sounded like a lot of money to make in a month; she was hoping to make that in a week. But she told him she would think about it.

When they pulled up to Stan's house, she noticed it was very nice, and the yard was well kept. He had a corner lot overlooking the city. She couldn't help but wonder how much it cost. With the kind of money he made, she found herself expecting his house to be even fancier. But if he gave a lot to nonprofits and was as selfless as he seemed to be, it actually made sense that he was living beneath his means. When they went inside, she put her bags in the family room, and they went into the study where Stan traded. Laura had seen it in videos online, but it was much more impressive in person. She looked down at his trading station and saw a pair of expensive looking watches sitting on the desk.

Stan noticed her looking at the watches and said, "Those were sent to me from a famous rapper friend of mine in L.A. He said he just felt like giving them to me."

"Wow," Laura said. "They are gorgeous." She exclaimed as she admired the decorative golden markings and sparkling stones surrounding the faces of the watches and contemplated how he'd even met a rapper in L.A.

"Yep, I don't even wear them, so I feel kinda guilty about it. They are worth more than a hundred thousand dollars each," Stan said. He then pulled out a shiny diamond necklace with very large stones from his top drawer. "He sent this too. I only wore it once to a business meeting. My business partner said, 'What in the world are you wearing, Stan?' with eyes as big as golf balls, and I said, 'My rapper friend gave it to me.' I didn't wear it after that." He laughed as he remembered that day. "Sometimes I feel like just sitting here at my desk, chair tilted back, with my arms behind my head, in a velour jogging suit and big spinner necklace around my neck and my sunglasses on, just to see what people would say when they walked in. They'd probably whisper to each other, 'What's up with Stan?' I'd just sit there for a while, staring at my charts, waiting to see if anyone would say anything. I think that would be funny."

Laura thought that Stan was a fun guy. He sure loved to laugh and tell jokes, and he obviously loved to watch human behavior. He told her about a time when he'd gone to Starbucks and bought a hundred-dollar gift card and gave it to the cashier. He told her to just keep paying for people's coffee until it ran out. Then he sat in the corner to watch people's reactions. He said one of the customers looked around and said something like, 'I won the coffee lottery?' He would laugh when he saw how confused yet delighted those people were. When he'd had enough fun from that, he went home.

Stan took Laura on a tour of the rest of his house and out to the garage, where he had several nice cars, including a Porsche and a Cobra and seventeen motorcycles. They were all custom-made. Stan mentioned that he liked to collect old motorcycles. Laura told Stan how much her husband would love to see them. Ryan was very much interested in motorcycles, race cars, and anything else that had a loud engine. They went back into the house and sat down at the trading station.

At that moment, his wife, Debbie, came in with a syringe on a tray with a sterile alcohol pad. "Here's your shot, honey," she said as she placed the tray on his trading desk and left the room.

"Ah, yes, my HCG shot. I just love giving them to myself. I don't know if I told you this, Laura, but I've been taking the HCG for two weeks now. I've lost ten pounds … and Debbie has lost over twenty. The first two days of the diet, you can eat whatever you want…it's actually encouraged, and then you can only eat…well, basically lettuce," Stan said.

Laura laughed. She knew the diet well. She knew you could only eat around five to seven hundred calories a day for the length of the diet. "Well, it seems to be working for you, as long as you are able to stand it," Laura said.

"I'd like it better if I could just keep repeating the first two days of the diet," Stan replied.

It was getting close to 10:00 p.m., and Stan began analyzing his charts. Laura got out her laptop and looked at her own charts. Stan seemed to be deep in thought. He told her they could review some trades together the following day. At 10:30 p.m., there was a knock on the door. It was the other visitor, named David, from Portland, Oregon. Stan introduced himself and Laura. They didn't really have time to talk, as other traders started filing in behind him. Laura was front and center, next to Stan.

She pulled up her trading platform. It was obvious she wouldn't need to worry about looking at her own charts, since Stan's were right in front of her, bigger than life, so she closed them out. A gentleman in his late fifties came in and sat down on the leather couch in the room next to the trading room and set up his computer and trading platform.

Stan said to him, "Hey, Paul, come and meet Laura."

"Hi, Laura," Paul said with a smile. Laura thought he seemed like a nice guy, based on the conference calls she had been on where Stan commended him on many occasions for helping people with their trading.

"Hi, Paul!" she exclaimed. "I'm glad I finally get to meet you. I've heard a lot about you."

Paul told her he was in the process of hanging up his career as a real estate agent in order to trade full time—or at least do full-time trading, depending on your definition of full time.

Stan said he only traded three or four hours per day, but he considered it full time.

"It's nice to meet you as well. Just let me know if you need help setting up any trades. In fact, I'll show you a couple of our private trades that Stan doesn't broadcast to everyone," he said.

"I'd really like that," Laura said. She was starting to feel very fortunate for making the decision to come to Olympia.

When the webinar began, she watched Stan put on his headset and was able to watch all of the comments roll in on his computer screen as people typed "Hello" or various questions. She had heard him respond to people's comments on countless occasions, but now she was on the other end of the webinar, and it was exciting to see it live.

"Okay, guys, you have my numbers tonight. I wouldn't trade the GBPUSD; it's already exceeded its average trading range for the day. I think we will see some downward movement on the EURUSD tonight," Stan said. Laura didn't know what the average trading range was, so she added it to her list of questions and promised herself to look it up in the morning. As Stan gave his analysis of the market, she decided to go sit with Paul. He made room for her on the couch and began to show her the special trade they were doing called the Power Cross. The five-minute chart was watched along with the five SMA, smooth moving average and twenty EMA, exponential moving average. When the cross occurred and several other criteria were met, the trade was entered, and a stop loss was placed above the corresponding high or low of the previous high or low, depending on if it was a buy or sell trade. This trade was done on any currency pair. She was excited about that trade, and as Paul reviewed the setups of previous nights, it was obvious that this was a winning trade, with a win-to-loss ratio of three to one.

While Laura was talking to Paul, Stan entered a trade with everyone due to a signal on a chart called the Big Mo, which Stan explained just meant "big momentum." It paid about sixteen pips before he got out of the trade.

"It's enough to buy pizza," Stan said. Some of the other people stayed in and ended up having to close out with only three pips before it went against them. That was equivalent to what the brokers made due to the spread. Stan had said many times he would never let the broker make more than he did in a trade. She noticed that Stan traded at least six accounts, but he never let anyone watch him take a trade. That was fine with Laura. *It's not anyone's business how much money Stan makes each time he takes a trade*, she thought. Before the webinar ended, Stan mentioned he would be interviewed by phone on *Fox Business News* the following week about the current state of the economy. Laura thought that was pretty cool.

At 1:00 a.m., Laura was exhausted. She was grateful that people were leaving. David stayed up and decided to watch the charts, and Laura went to the family room to sleep on the couch. At about 5:00 a.m., she woke up to find David still watching the charts. David said he was going to be there for the next couple of days to learn more from Stan in person and that he was able to make a few successful trades but still had some questions. Stan came into the room to look at his charts as well. At about seven o'clock, Stan asked if they wanted to go to Starbucks. David and Laura said yes in unison.

A few hours of that day were spent with Stan reviewing some of his different trading strategies with Laura and David. Laura still didn't feel like she was getting it. She wasn't sure about David. He didn't say too much; he just kept studying his charts. Stan mentioned to Laura that he knew a couple of traders from Chico. Stan was big on starting local trading clubs. She took down their information, and Stan offered to give one of them a call to introduce her. She was introduced to Cameron briefly on the phone and one of his trading partner named Calvin, who said, "Everyone calls me Cal." They invited her to come by once she returned to Chico. She accepted the invitation. She spent most of the rest of the day sleeping.

The next trading session was as uneventful as the first one. Dan mentioned a special machine called the Power Nap. "And no, it was not named after me," he had said. When you put on the headphones and listened to something like white noise for about twenty minutes, it was supposed to make you feel like you got five hours of sleep. *Now that sounds like a miracle*, Laura had thought. She knew she would be purchasing one of those when she got back home. Evidently, Stan didn't need as much sleep as the average person. Laura, on the other hand, had continued to struggle with the lack of sleep. She realized that even though she had made a few pips, she still didn't see how she could make the pips off Stan's numbers without being up all night to watch the charts. She hoped meeting the traders in Chico would help. She couldn't wait to see how they were doing.

The next morning Stan drove Laura to the airport. With her sleep/wake cycle being disrupted, and Ryan being asleep when she was awake, she hadn't told Ryan too much about her experience. She was glad to go home so she could tell him about Stan. She thanked Stan and told him she would talk to Ryan about the robot fund he had. She had given it a second thought and realized that was actually a very good return compared to most other kinds of investments. It ended up being 60 percent a year, she estimated.

When she disembarked the plane, she found Ryan waiting for her at the security exit.

"Hi, honey. Happy birthday! Did you have a good trip?" he said as he gave her a kiss and a hug and a big bouquet of Gerbera daisies—her favorite.

"Oh, yes. I can't wait to tell you all about it," she said. "But I'm glad to be back." On the way home, she shared with Ryan about the experience and the people she'd met, along with the opportunity that Stan offered with the robot fund.

"What are you saying, Laura? Do you think you are going to be able to trade, or are you saying you want to put some money into Stan's fund?" Ryan asked.

"I think it would be a good idea, Ryan. It's a guaranteed 4 percent a month. If you think about it, that's a great return—around 60 percent a year."

"If you think it's a good idea … we should pray about it first," he said.

"Well, I'll give it a little longer and see how my own trading goes," she said.

Ryan nodded in agreement. "When we get home, we can change for dinner. We are heading to your favorite restaurant, Anselmo's. Our reservations are at seven," Ryan exclaimed.

Laura clapped her hands together and said in an excited whisper, "Yes!"

LAURA'S CELL PHONE RANG AS she was walking towards her front door.

"Hello?" Laura said.

"Hello, Laura, this is Cal."

Laura was surprised; she hadn't expected him to call so soon.

"Is this a good time to call? I know you mentioned you would be getting home today," he said.

"Oh, yes, I was just walking up to my front door," she said. She had to wait outside because she knew if she opened the door, the dogs would bark, and she wouldn't be able to hear Cal.

"Good. I'm calling to see if you and your husband want to come by Monday night. Cameron and I are going to be trading the London session with Stan and listening to his webinar. We can analyze the charts together and trade live with Stan."

"Oh, that actually sounds great, I could use the support. Where do you live?"

After Cal gave her directions, she hung up the phone and ceremoniously flung open her front door in order to greet the dogs.

"Who was that?" Ryan asked as he walked in the door. He had been in the garage and had emerged just in time to hear her say good-bye to someone.

"Oh, that was Cal. He and another guy named Cameron are traders that know Stan and trade with him on his webinars. Cal lives only five minutes away from us. Isn't that cool? He invited us over to trade Monday night for the London session."

"I'll have to take a nap; that's for sure," Ryan said. He loved to take naps to recharge his batteries, but in this case, it was going to be vital for him.

"Speaking of naps, I learned about something called a Power Nap. It gives you five hours of sleep in twenty minutes. Stan told me about it. I definitely want to buy one," she said.

"Think we can get it by Monday?" Ryan asked. Laura just laughed.

That night they had a great dinner at Anselmo's Vineyard. Laura loved the food and the beautiful setting. Ryan had asked the wait staff to put them in the special room with a large picture window overlooking the vineyard. After dinner, on the way home, Laura fell asleep in the car. Ryan woke her up and led her to bed, where she promptly fell back asleep.

When Monday evening came, Laura was excited to meet Cal and Cameron. After dinner, she and Ryan took a nap to prepare for the late night. She didn't have the Power Nap machine yet, but she had placed the order. In the meantime, she bought some 5-Hour Energy drink shots. Stan had also recommended them to her. She got it at the local Big Lots. She read the ingredients and immediately had some reservations about it. She had noticed previously that the caffeine in that small shot-sized container was enough to cause her heart to race. That never happened when she drank coffee, so she knew it had a hefty dose. *This probably isn't the most healthful thing for my body,* she thought. But she knew she needed an extra boost to get her through the night.

After their naps, Laura and Ryan each took a 5-Hour Energy shot. They got into the car and headed over to Cal's house. When they pulled up to the house, they noticed the front door was wide open, and Cal was inside, waiting for them. Laura and Ryan walked up the walkway and weren't sure if they should just walk in or knock.

"Cal?" Laura called out.

"Oh, hey!" Cal smiled and walked quickly toward his front door. "How are you guys? You must be Ryan. I'm Cal." He extended his hand toward Ryan. He then shook Laura's hand and said, "Come in. Cameron is in the kitchen. Cameron? Laura and Ryan are here." Laura noticed that Cal was drinking a large mug of coffee and had an espresso machine in his kitchen with several other mugs on the kitchen island.

"Hi, Cameron," Laura and Ryan said in unison.

Cameron looked to be in his early twenties. He was thin and had very short whitish-blond hair and a boyish face. He mentioned that he was in the worship band at church. He said that Cal and he went to the same church. Cal looked to be in his late forties but in good shape. He had tan skin and medium-long brown hair. He was wearing a V-neck light blue T-shirt and khaki shorts. He said that his wife and two sons were in L.A. His younger son, Lance, was a child actor; he was ten. Cal excitedly told them that Lance was currently in a national Olive Garden commercial.

"I was donating blood the other day, and my son's commercial came on in the lobby area, and I pointed at the TV and said to the man standing next to me in line, 'There's my son!'" Cal went on to talk about how Lance had made the choice to move to L. A. for more acting opportunities. He was going to appear on the latest episode of *Childhood Sweethearts*, a popular sitcom. It was obvious to Laura that Cal was very proud of his son. His older son was sixteen and was also in L.A., working on the set of the show. He was trying to break into the business as well. Laura and Ryan just smiled. They didn't really feel inclined to talk as Cal was doing a great job carrying on the conversation for all of them. Cal offered them espressos, which they both accepted.

"I only use stevia for a sweetener, along with half-and-half," he said.

"That's perfect," Laura said. They also tried to stay away from sugar and used stevia when they could. Laura didn't think it tasted very good in certain drinks—like iced tea, for example—but it tasted just fine in coffee. Cal then led them into a dimly lit study, which was the room immediately off of the entrance.

"And here is my trading station!" Cal said excitedly. He had five large monitors for trading and went into a long discussion of how he purchased and set up each monitor a certain way to have certain charting packages displayed at strategic places for his viewing. He then went into a detailed description of using a special broker, which allowed him to have access to certain charts for free. He was fortunate to get a chart of the Dollar Index, for which most people had to pay a fee. As Laura and Ryan were taking it all in, they noticed that it was getting close to the live trading session with Stan. Laura mentioned this to Cal, who logged into the webinar for her.

"I don't really listen to too much of Stan, just the first ten minutes or so, where he gives his analysis of the market," Cal said. As the webinar began, Cal continued to talk as well and show Laura the new signal Cameron and he were looking at to enter a trade. Cal also remarked that if Stan confirmed that the euro was headed down, they most likely would be looking to enter the trade tonight. Laura didn't want to miss the action, so she listened along with Cal and Cameron to see what Stan thought of the market.

"Well, guys, I think I'm entering my sell numbers tonight. It looks like the euro may be headed down with the reports coming out," Stan said. Cal, Cameron, and Laura looked at each other and smiled. In the meantime, Ryan was fast asleep on the couch in the living room.

"Look at the Kelpie forming on the one-hour chart, four-hour chart, and daily chart! You can't have a better signal than that!" Cal said.

"Well, the market just opened. Shouldn't we give it some time?" Laura asked. She had learned her lesson from trying to enter trades too early in the London session.

"We might miss out if we don't enter it before the report," Cal said. "Cameron and I are going to take the trade." Laura decided she would enter it also. "On the count of three: one, two ... three!" Cal said. They all pushed their Sell buttons in unison. The GDP for the United States came out thirty minutes later. It was better than predicted for the United States, and the USD started to rise, and they all high-fived each other and laughed.

"How long are you planning to stay in the trade?" Laura asked.

"Not sure. I'll probably take forty pips," Cal said. Then, after ten minutes of watching the euro go down, the euro started to rise quickly with some momentum. As they sat there in utter amazement, the roughly twenty-five pips of profit they had quickly came back to zero and continued to make their accounts sink further as the euro kept rising. All of a sudden, what was a twenty-five-pip profit for Laura became a twenty-five-pip loss. She continued to watch the chart to look for any sign of rebound.

"It should turn back around soon. This is just a fake-out," Cal said. They sat and watched their charts closely for any sign of a turnaround. Laura was getting nervous. She couldn't help but notice the velocity with which her trade was now flying in the opposite direction! Now the trade was sixty pips in the hole. *Great* she thought. *My first trade with Cal and Cameron, and it's a bad one. I should just get out now and take the loss.* But Laura couldn't bring herself to close out the trade. She was getting very tired, and it was 2:00 a.m. She wasn't looking forward to working tomorrow. She knew how hard it was to see patients when she was sleep-deprived. *After all, that's what my residency was all about*, she thought. It was crazy. Sleep deprivation was bad enough, but add the insult of losing money as well, and it was just too much to bear.

"Okay, I think it's time for Ryan and me to go home," Laura said.

"Just call me tomorrow, and we can review the trade. I'm staying in because I think it's going to turn around. We can cost average and make a great return when it does turn around," Cal said.

Laura thought that might be a good idea, but she was too tired to really think about it. She woke up Ryan and they headed out the door. "It was nice to meet you guys," she said.

"Yes, I'm glad we have a new trader to work with us," Cameron said.

"Be careful on the way home. Good night," Cal said.

"Good night," Laura said. When they got in the car, Ryan had a hard time keeping his eyes open, so they turned up the radio and opened the windows.

"I can't wait to go to sleep," Ryan said. Laura just closed her eyes.

The next morning Laura got up and briefly looked at her charts. She didn't have enough time to really study her charts, but she did notice the glaring deficit that her account had gotten into overnight. *I can't believe this.* She had to get to work, so she quickly loaded up her laptop and kissed Ryan good-bye. At work, she watched the charts, hoping for a turnaround. But now a new thought had come up. Seeing that the account was over one hundred pips in the hole, perhaps this would be a good time to sell again, so as to cost average. She realized, though, that if she did that, she would be overleveraged. *I think I'll wait until it's at least 150 pips in the hole*, she thought. A few nights later Laura sat by the television to wait for Stan's interview on Fox. It was a short interview, and Stan quickly gave his opinion on where the dollar was going and how the current administration was devaluing the dollar. Laura listened intently. She knew Stan was trying to grow his company and being on *Fox Business News* was a great way to do that.

About two weeks later, Laura, Cal, and Cameron got together to talk about trading. They went over some historical charts in order to test a new strategy. They didn't talk about the trade that they had gotten into two weeks earlier. It was a touchy subject, now that it was 250 pips in the hole. Laura made the mistake of selling again when she was two hundred pips in the hole, and now that new trade was also in the hole. While they were reviewing the new strategy, Laura made the decision to invest with Stan. She couldn't wait much longer; she was getting very concerned about her own trading success.

When she got home that night, she told Ryan what she wanted to do.

"How much do you want to put in to his account?" He asked.

"I was thinking of putting in eighty thousand dollars. We could just borrow it and put it in for a while. The more we put in, the quicker it will grow," she said. She had been reading Stan's dad's books on faith and felt that Stan had a special gift. She even read about a time when his dad had been given a prophecy about having millions of dollars coming his way. She was sure that it was fulfilled in Stan's trading success.

"We could even borrow from my brother, Barry," she said. "He is always looking for a way to make a profit. We could offer him 10–15 percent per year and keep the rest, since we would be the ones taking all of the risk."

Ryan thought about it for a while. "Well, I guess we could do that. Have you prayed about it?" He asked.

"Yes, I feel like we should do this."

"I'm not really getting a sense of whether we should or shouldn't, but if you are, then I think it's okay to do it."

"I also think we should talk to our friends Jan and Joshua about borrowing money from them and see if they want to earn 10 percent return on their money."

"Yeah, let's see if they are interested. I know they wouldn't mind making extra money since they are retired. I'll talk to Josh tomorrow," Ryan said.

"I'll let Stan know," she said.

CHAPTER 5

THE NEXT MONTH WAS RATHER uneventful in the FOREX trading world for Laura. She was still in that "bad trade," as she referred to it when talking to Ryan, and had closed out some of her lots that were in the hole over three hundred pips. She figured by closing out the trades a little at a time, she wouldn't feel as bad about taking the loss as she would have if she just closed them all out at once. She really regretted getting into that trade in the first place and realized it was hindering her ability to keep trading because she didn't want to be overleveraged. She didn't want to keep repeating the same trading mistakes. She also found that there was a new law in trading now. She wouldn't be able to buy and sell the same currency pair at the same time, at least not if she traded a US account. At some point, she was going to have to close out some trades. She knew she had the option of adding more money to her account. *At least I have the money in the account with Stan,* she thought.

Laura had called Stan last month and had invested the eighty thousand dollars in his account. She had deposited it in an account held by S & S Investments at the local Chase bank. Stan had provided the account numbers. She was going to invest another hundred thousand dollars that she had borrowed from her brother. She had agreed to give him back 15 percent total return on his money in one year. She was excited to see the investment grow. Stan e-mailed Laura her total account balance at the end of the month. He told her she could withdraw money whenever she wanted it. She, of course, had no desire to withdraw anything for at least one year. She wanted the quickest return possible. Ryan had talked to Joshua and Jan, and they were interested in the investment but didn't have a lot of money to invest, so they were going to wait.

In August, Stan stopped trading for one month. He did this every year. He didn't really see too many trading opportunities in the summer when there was less trading volume. Laura asked if the robot account was affected due to the lowered volume. Stan assured her that it really didn't have an impact on the robot fund.

"That account is a steady earner," he said.

Laura was glad that she could take a break for the month of August. She was looking forward to catching up on her sleep.

In September, Laura got back on the webinars with Stan. She had gone over to Cal's house a couple of times to continue to test other strategies for trading. She finally had to close out of her other "bad trade" due to the new laws coming into effect in the United States. She lost a couple of thousand dollars, but she chalked it up to "pip tuition", as Stan would say. She had kept in touch with Paul throughout her short trading career and decided to give him a call to ask for advice on other trading strategies. Paul had provided some new charts and a strategy that he and a few other traders were currently using to trade. She decided that at some point she would try trading with Paul on the phone at night during the webinars. For the rest of the month, she had had successful trades, but overall, she was still not profitable.

At the beginning of October, Stan had mentioned his live Boot Camp trading seminar. She had thought it would be great to meet and trade live with other traders around the United States and also out of the country. Stan started advertising his Boot Camp and even did a short YouTube video to promote it. It was going to be in Olympia Washington, in mid-November.

One day Laura asked Ryan, "Do you think I could go to Boot Camp? It's only for two days?"

"It's fine with me. I just wish I could go with you, but I need to stay and work," he said.

"I know, honey, but I'll be fine. I think Cal is going too."

"Sounds good, babe." Ryan was easygoing about Laura's decisions. He knew she was very wise about her choices.

Stan continued to promote the Boot Camp on his webinar. "I'll be talking a lot about the psychology of trading. Trading is really all about psychology, and, of course, probabilities. Trading is 99 percent mental attitude and 1 percent math. So I will be talking about that, along with goal setting. Did you know less than 3 percent of the population has a goal statement? We'll be talking about that. There are only a few spots left, by the way, so if you still want to go to Boot Camp, please let us know. You won't want to miss it."

Someone typed in to ask where it was going to be held. Stan said it was supposed to be at his local church, the Rock Church, but due to a scheduling conflict, he decided to move it to a conference room at the local casino.

That struck Laura as a huge contrast. *Guess it really doesn't make a difference*, she thought. Several people agreed with Laura, as the comments they typed in to Stan reflected her sentiment. She knew that Cal was going to the seminar, as was Paul. She couldn't wait to see Paul again to ask him about his new trading strategies in person.

The morning of the seminar, Laura boarded her plane. That same morning, 350 other traders from all over the United States and several other countries also made their respective journeys to Olympia, Washington. There was a big snowstorm in Olympia the day before, and some of the roads were still very snowy, with small mountains of snow plowed to each side of the icy road. When she arrived, she grabbed her suitcase and made her way outside to the rental car shuttle bus and was glad to see it was pulling up as she walked out to the curb. She found herself shivering on the shuttle and was glad to finally make it into the rental car building. Finally, after taking care of the paperwork, Laura got into her rental car and drove to the hotel. A lot of traders, including Cal, were staying at her hotel, since they were given a group discount. When she walked into the Best Western lobby, she saw there was a Starbucks. Laura smiled. She would definitely be a patron there very soon. She decided to go to her room first to lie down for a few minutes before showering and changing. After reviving herself, she headed down to the lobby to grab a snack and her favorite brew, and she ran into Cal who was standing in line.

"Hi, Laura. How are you?"

"I'm good, Cal. It's good to see you. Is Cameron also here?"

"No, he didn't have the money for the trip, unfortunately."

"Oh, that's too bad," Laura said. Changing the subject, she added, "I can't believe how much snow they've gotten here! It's crazy. I'm glad it doesn't snow in Chico like this."

"If you want, we can drive together."

"That sounds good. Thank you," Laura said as Cal put half-and-half into his coffee.

Laura ordered a double espresso and a yogurt parfait. After grabbing a napkin, Laura buttoned up her coat, and they headed out to the parking lot.

"I'll pull my car around; you can wait here," he said as he ran to get his car. Laura nodded in agreement. Soon, they were on the road.

The distance to the casino was only five miles, but with the treacherous roads combined with Cal's style of driving, Laura had a cramp in her right hand from gripping the strap above the passenger car door while Cal weaved through traffic like he was driving a stock car around a race track, and was trying to overtake the front runner. *Note to self, never drive with Cal again, anywhere!* When they arrived, the parking lot was packed. They found a parking space far away from the entrance. Laura slowly loosened her grip on the door strap and they walked into the casino lobby and saw a sign welcoming the PowersFx traders to Boot Camp. They proceeded to follow the signs to the conference room and found the sign-in table.

"Welcome to Boot Camp. I'm Sally," a young lady in her early thirties said to them as she smiled. She was Stan's secretary.

As she was preparing their name tags, Paul walked up to Laura and said, "Well, hello, Laura. It's good to see you again."

"Hi, Paul. How are you?" She said as she gave him a hug. "This is my trading friend from Chico, Cal."

"Hi, Cal."

"Nice to meet you. Laura has mentioned that you are a pretty good trader."

"It's been going well," Paul said. He remembered and said, "Hey, that reminds me Laura … I've got a pretty good new trade to show you. We've been trading it for a month now, and we are seeing a good return."

"Great. I can't wait to look at that with you!"

"Me too," Cal said.

"Here are your name tags, Laura and Cal. Enjoy the seminar!" Sally said. Paul pointed out a few other people with whom he traded. He also pointed out the tech guy, Aaron, who made sure all of the webinars ran smoothly. He was speaking with Stan at the front of the room about his

PowerPoint presentation. Laura recognized a few of the other traders from Stan's house during the webinar.

Laura and Cal looked around the conference room, and Laura quickly realized she was in the minority. She was one of only five women in a room of about two hundred people. It appeared to her that at least two of the women were just accompanying their husbands, who were the traders.

"Hey, Laura, I'm going to go talk to a few traders. I'll come find you. Could you please just save me a seat?" Cal said.

"No problem. I'm going to go save two seats close to Paul if I can."

At 7:00 p.m. on the dot, Stan spoke into his microphone. He was wearing a state-of-the-art headset microphone so he could easily manage his PowerPoint slides. He was dressed in a nice button-down dark purple shirt and blue jeans. His wife, Debbie, and his two sons were sitting in the back of the room at a round table, watching Stan as well. To Laura, it looked like Debbie was knitting some kind of scarf. She had her dog, Mocha, with her; the dog was wearing a pink bow and lying on her special pink heart-shaped dog bed. Laura hadn't been able to locate a seat near Paul, so she found two seats near the back of the room. She quickly sat down just in time for Stan's welcoming remarks.

"Good evening, traders!" Stan said. The microphone reverberated, and Laura involuntarily put her hands to her ears. She noticed several others doing the same thing out of the corner of her eye. Aaron acted quickly and adjusted the sound for Stan.

"Wow, that was a thunderous beginning," Stan proclaimed. Everyone applauded for Stan. A lot of the people stood up. The applause went on for a full minute before he was able to speak and be heard again.

"I'm honored ... please, have a seat," Stan said as he beckoned for them to sit by raising up his hands and making a downward motion. "Thank you, thank you."

Finally, everyone took their seats in anticipation of what was to come next.

"Okay, everyone. Thank you for being here tonight. I want everyone to know that this is one big family. This is a safe environment, so everything you say here is held in confidence. How many of you have ever margined an account?" Several people raised their hands. "Did you know that the average person has margined their account five times?" he asked. Stan laughed as he heard someone remark, "Only one more to go!" Everyone else laughed as well.

"I want to start by saying, welcome to the top 5 percent of the world. Give yourselves a hand. Not many people take the time to attend seminars to change their lives. I have a tip for you: take something that you learn here and apply it out there. Only 2 percent of people do. We won't change *the* world until we change *our* world. One of my goals is to give one billion dollars to charity, and I say that as often as I can. I'm on my way. If I have to do it by myself, it might be tough—or not. But it would be much easier if I had a hundred thousand people to do it with me. What if we picked a night and I called up, let's say, two thousand of my favorite people and asked for forty-five minutes of your trading time? And whatever we make, we give away. We may only make enough for pizza, or we may make one million dollars—enough to build one hundred water wells in Africa or a Bible school. We've done it already with a group of thirty people and gave it away.

"Did you know the average person lives on about forty thousand dollars a year in retirement? One-third of that money goes to health care. Obviously, we are not talking fat living on the Riviera. I was at the bank the other day, and I saw a sign that read 'Jumbo five-year CD, 1.75 percent.' I thought, 'Is that decimal in the wrong place? Could that be right?' Americans live on 113 percent of their income. Most people go to work for eight hours and are away from their families all day for about a hundred bucks. They used to say not to put your money into the stock market at age seventy. Now they are saying put nothing into stocks after age sixty. I have a quote for you—it's one of my favorites:

"'On the whole, though, we are a society of notoriously numb people— lonely, bored, dependent people who are happy only when we have killed the time we are trying so hard to save. We worry constantly about making a living, but rarely about making a life. In our businesses and financial markets across the country, people scramble frantically trying to make a killing, but end up instead, killing their lives.' That's from *Repacking Your Bags* by David A. Shapiro."

"It makes you think, doesn't it? We plan our vacations, but we don't really plan our lives. I don't take a vacation. Vacate means 'to get away from.' I'm not trying to get away. I call it a holiday. If you want to be successful, do what successful people do. It's a formula. You will get the same results. I learned the formula ten years ago, and it revolutionized my life."

"Money is a tool. Money is not good or bad. True or false? A hammer is a tool. It can be used to build a house or crush a skull. What's the difference? The hand holding it. Money doesn't change people; it makes you bigger than what you currently are: jerk with a nickel … big jerk with a million; good with no money … fantastic with a bunch. If you've never had money, you won't know what to do with it when you get it. So you get a money manager, who gives you a hundred thousand dollars and say, 'Do whatever you want with it'. Go buy your electric sweater. Why? To get it out of your system."

"What would you do if you knew you couldn't fail? What would you do if money no longer had value? I don't need to know the answer; you do. We always tell ourselves stories. We lie to ourselves. I decided if I was going to lie to myself, I was going to make sure the lie served me. Because … evidently … I don't know the difference." A few people laughed at this statement, but otherwise everyone was listening intently to Stan. "I just look in the mirror and say, I'm going to go get some pips, and then I do."

People were nodding their heads in agreement with Stan's statements.

"Let's take a fifteen-minute break and then get back to it. I want to stay on schedule, so we will be starting exactly at 8:15 p.m.," Stan said.

Laura got up and stretched her arms up over her head. She leaned over and asked Cal, "Do you want to go find some coffee somewhere?"

"I want to go talk to Stan."

"Okay, then, I'll be right back," she said. As she was walking out of the room, she ran into Paul, who was talking with a few other traders.

"Hey, Laura, these are my friends Joey and Natalie Grimm. We trade together most nights on the phone."

"Oh, great, it's nice to meet you. I can't wait to try out some of your new trades."

"You should trade with us on the phone," Natalie said.

"I'd love to. I'm hoping to go over some trades with Paul tomorrow," Laura said.

"That sounds good," Joey said.

"Well, I'm going to go see if I can find some coffee," Laura said.

At precisely 8:15 p.m., the lights dimmed and then brightened two times.

"Welcome back everyone. Let's get started. I'd like to talk about goals. We were created to be successful, but we are programmed for defeat by our environment. What is your purpose? What is important to you? I don't spend time with my family; I invest time. I invest in people and opportunities. I'm an investor. When you invest, there is an expectation for return. In the business world, it's called ROI, or return on investment. For trading, the first things you need are rules. You have to have rules. The market is relentless. Learn to respect the market. You have to develop a strategy. The FOREX world is powerful. You have to have correct money management as well. We always talk in pip and percentages. If I told you guys what I made in a day, I'd wet my pants, so I don't know what it would do to you. Sit down to look for a trade, not to trade. Set your goals for a day, and stop trading when you get your goal. Take responsibility for your trading decisions. You need to develop a goal statement. How many people in the room have a goal statement?" Stan looked around the room and saw seven hands.

"So, just seven out of two hundred in this room. I encourage you to write down everything you want. First, write down the top ten things, and then the one thing. You have to know what you want. Someone will fill in your details if you don't. Let me ask you a question: do dogs like bones? If I put a steak on one side of the kitchen and bones on the other, which does the dog choose? I'm going to suggest that dogs like steaks, not bones. If they could set the table, they would get the steaks, and we would get the bones. They settle for bones." Stan paused for effect before continuing. "What are your dreams? What are you settling for? Who are your friends? Would you like some new ones?"

Laura noticed that several people laughed at that remark.

"I had this 'friend' once. I actually called him the 'black-sucking-hole of the universe.' He was so negative. I called him one day and said, 'Greg, can you buy me coffee?' I wasn't going to buy him coffee. He said, 'I guess. Of course you're going to say that—like I've got all the money.' When we met at the coffee shop, I said to him, 'I've noticed that you are a black-sucking-hole and you destroy everything around you. I'm choosing not to be destroyed.' He said, 'Yeah, everyone gives up on me sooner or later.' That's called pity. He was a zero at every level. I went to my car and drove away, feeling great. So measure the people around you that you call friends. I think you only need six—to carry the box when you are done." Stan paused to let that sentiment float in the room for several seconds, and then he continued.

"You can start again. We lived on credit cards for two years after coming off of ministry. We had dug a financial hole. Bill collectors used to carpool to our house. I'd get calls. Boy, those people like to scream. I'd say, 'Listen, I know that you're paid to scream at me. I have a system. I get a lot of bills right now, and I just throw them in a big box. At the end of the month, I take out three and pay them. So if you scream at me, I'm not going to put you in the box. Your choice.' So I've had struggles too. I'm an anomaly in the system. But I'm not bulletproof—good looking but not bulletproof," he said. People laughed around the room.

"Well, I think that's a good place to stop for the evening," Stan said. Everyone stood up and started clapping for Stan and cheering. It was 9:00 p.m., and Laura waited for the applause to die down, leaned over to Cal, and said, "I can't wait to get back to the hotel. It's been a long day."

"Yes, me too, but I just want to go talk to one more person before we go," he said.

Laura nodded and stayed seated while Cal spoke to a few other people for ten minutes. She was glad when she saw him come back to where she was sitting, but was dreading the drive back to the hotel.

On the way back, Laura and Cal spoke about the seminar. Laura couldn't help but wonder in the back of her mind if Stan was going to teach more on the technicalities of trading. So far it seemed like a motivational seminar. She enjoyed listening to Stan, but she just wanted more information and teaching on trading.

When they got to the hotel, Cal dropped her off at the entrance. "We can meet down here in the morning and leave together, if you want," he said.

"I'm not sure exactly when I'll be leaving in the morning, I'll just meet you there. Have a good night," Laura said quickly as she walked toward the hotel entrance.

The next day at the seminar Laura arrived a few minutes early to be able to get a better seat upfront by Paul and his group of traders. Cal had also arrived early and was already sitting with Paul. Stan began promptly at 9:00 a.m.

"Good morning, everyone. I hope you had the chance to think about what I said last night. I am the son of a motivational speaker. I don't really believe in motivational speaking, but I believe in my dad. He made us write a mission statement to be able to get our allowance. I don't want this seminar to be just another seminar that you forget by next week. I want you to really think about who you are and who you want to become." After speaking for another hour, Stan gave everyone a ten-minute break and then began speaking again. By lunchtime, Laura was starving. When they were dismissed for lunch, Paul, Laura, Cal, and the Grimms went to lunch together to discuss trading strategies. Before lunch, Stan had asked people to write down questions on a piece of paper for him to read in the afternoon session. The person whose question was chosen to be read would win a trip with Stan to trade live on his yacht. Laura couldn't really think of any good questions so she decided not to enter the contest.

"Hey, guys, let's eat downstairs at the casino restaurant so we have more time to discuss trades," Paul said.

"Sounds like a plan," Laura and Natalie said in unison and laughed.

When everyone got their meals, Paul pulled out his laptop to review several new trades.

"So here is the latest trade we are doing," Paul said.

Laura took notes as Paul explained the nuances of the trade using the five and twelve EMAs on the five-minute chart, along with several other indicators, including the MACD (Moving Average Convergence Divergence). It appeared to be working well, as Paul showed them the back-testing results.

"Stan is using this trade now, and I think he is going to forward test it a little longer before introducing it to the group. But he said he's already made thousands of dollars with it in the last week," Paul said.

Wow, Laura thought. *I'm definitely going to have to work with this new trade.* "I'm excited to try it out!" Laura remarked.

After lunch, they all headed back to the conference room, while Stan was getting ready to speak again. After everyone quieted down and took their seats, Stan said, "Okay, everyone, we are getting into the final session. But before I begin I just want to congratulate Mike Olson, who is the winner of the live trading session on my yacht," Stan said. "He asked a great question about the Fibonacci numbers and Fibonacci extensions. So, this afternoon I'd like to discuss how to trade with Fibonacci numbers using different time frames."

Laura actually got excited and took out her notebook to take more notes. She was glad he was finally getting into technical trading. Stan began by showing his charts on the big screen and going through the current charts on the EURUSD. He went into a fifteen-minute discussion on how to use the Fibonacci indicator. When he finished, several people raised their hands and asked questions. Stan was very good at explaining the strategy behind the Fibonacci. Laura thought that this session was the most helpful to her for trading. She wished he had spent more time on the technicals. Stan moved onto the topic of the red reports and the fundamental type of trader versus the technical trader. At 3:00 p.m., Stan wrapped up the seminar.

"Thank you all for coming this weekend. Everyone have a safe trip home, and we will be putting out the numbers tomorrow afternoon as usual for the Sunday night and early Monday morning sessions."

Everyone gave one final standing ovation and then began to clear out of the room. A lot of the traders exchanged contact information with each other. Laura went up to the front of the room to say thank you to Stan. He thanked her for coming and gave her a hug to say good-bye. She told him she planned to be one of his Birth of a Million traders by next year. Stan agreed with her. Laura made sure that Paul had her information as well before heading back to the hotel and to the airport.

While packing up his equipment for the drive home, Stan had some time to reflect on the weekend after saying good-bye to Laura. He had been a little nervous about this Boot Camp and before each presentation had nonchalantly looked around the room for people who seemed out of place. He was starting to feel like a trapped animal, not only at this conference but even while he was at home or church. Besides that, he couldn't quite get rid of the migraine that had plagued him all weekend.

But as usual, Stan thought to himself, *The show must go on.*

CHAPTER 6

During the week following Boot Camp, Stan invited all of the traders online to his home for a Christmas party.

"Hey, everyone, we are having a small get-together at my house in two weeks to celebrate Christmas. Please come and bring your family, if you would like. We'll have some good food and just hang out," Stan said. Then Laura heard him ask Debbie in the background what they would be having to eat. Debbie said it would be catered by some friends of hers.

"Would you like us to bring anything, Stan?" asked Eric, a fellow trader.

"No need; just come hungry."

Laura thought this would be fun to do, even though it was a long drive to Olympia from their home. The next day she asked Ryan if he would like to go.

"Sure, I don't mind driving. We have four-wheel drive, so it should be fine," he said. Ryan was excited to finally meet Stan in person … and to see his cool motorcycles that Laura told him about. Stan seemed like the kind of guy that Ryan could hang out with.

"I'll ask Cal if he is planning to go," Laura said. "Maybe we can all go together."

The day before Stan's Christmas party, there was a blizzard that delivered twelve inches of snow in the Northwest. Laura and Ryan weren't going to let the weather change their plans, but Cal and his family decided to stay home. They left at 6:00 a.m. on the day of the party. When they passed the Washington State line they got into a very big snowstorm that reduced Ryan's visibility drastically. They were driving over sheets of ice. To Laura's left, up ahead by twenty-five yards, there was a large object on the side of the road. As they got closer, they saw an eighteen-wheeler overturned. To the right there were several pickup trucks stuck in the snow. The snow kept pouring down, and Laura and Ryan were both praying to get there without getting into an accident. She was surprised that they were able to maintain traction on the icy road. When they finally pulled into Stan's driveway, they both breathed a sigh of relief and Ryan said, "Thank the Lord!" Stan's sons were outside in the driveway, directing them where to park.

The house looked beautiful with its shining white Christmas lights lining the driveway and the icicle lights hanging from the roof edge. There was a massive Christmas tree in the front window adorned with gold trim and beautiful yellow lights and topped with a sparkling white star. As they got closer they could see that the tips of the branches were flocked with white "snow," and large red felt bows dotted the tree.

When they got inside they immediately felt warm and welcome. People were laughing and chatting while "Jingle Bells" played in the background. In one corner, people were playing Charades.

Just as they were about to see what kind of food was being served, Stan walked around the corner from the trading room and welcomed Laura with a big hug.

"This must be your husband … Ryan, was it?" Stan asked with a huge smile on his face.

Ryan nodded and replied, "Yes, it's great to finally meet you. Thank you so much for inviting us."

"Sure, I'm just glad you could come. How was the trip from the airport?"

"Oh, we didn't fly; we drove," Ryan said.

"What?" Stan raised his eyebrows in disbelief. "I have friends who live five minutes away who didn't want to come out in this storm, let alone twelve hours!" He laughed, shaking his head.

"It wasn't that bad," Laura said.

"Well, since you guys came such a long way, I'm going to give you a personal trading session, Laura, whenever you would like."

Laura smiled. "Awesome."

"Why don't you guys get some food? You must be hungry."

"Sure thing," Ryan responded as they walked to the kitchen. Paul was there with his wife, eating some chocolate-covered bacon, when he saw Laura walk in.

"Hey, Laura, it's good to see you again. Is this Ryan?"

"Yes, this is the one and only," she responded.

"Nice to meet you. This is my wife, Alex. Let me know if you want me to review any trades with you while you are here. I think Stan is giving a few of us some pointers for what may happen to the euro in the next few weeks."

"Hi, Alex, it's nice to meet you … and that sounds great, Paul," she said. She was very glad she had come to this event. Ryan also seemed to be enjoying himself.

Ryan and Laura sat down to eat their plates of food in the study. Ryan had to try the chocolate-covered bacon since he had never had it before. It was surprisingly good. He offered a bite to Laura, who tried it without hesitation.

"Wow, I never would have thought that this would taste good, but somehow it does!"

Stan came into the study and sat down with them and asked them about their financial goals. He stressed the importance of her perseverance as a trader but mentioned that the robot fund was a great thing to fall back on in the meantime. Laura mentioned that she had a few friends who might be interested in putting money into his fund as well.

"The only ones who lose at FOREX are the ones who give up," Stan said and then changed the subject. "Hey, let me show you something." He turned to his desk and brought out his wallet, which turned out to be a gun, just shaped like a wallet. "If someone ever holds me up at gunpoint and asks for my wallet, I'll have a surprise for them," he said.

Laura wasn't that crazy about guns, but it was a cool idea, she thought.

"Wow! Does that work?" Ryan asked.

"Of course," Stan responded; then, looking like a light bulb had gone off in his brain, he added, "Hey, Ryan, Laura said you like motorcycles. Would you like to see mine?"

"What a dumb question," Ryan said with a smile.

Thirty minutes later, both Ryan and Stan returned from the garage. Ryan had seen some pretty cool bikes in his lifetime, but not as many in the same room. Ryan told Laura that Stan had offered to take him out on the bikes in the spring. Laura knew that would be fun for him, although she wasn't exactly thrilled with the idea. She didn't feel that motorcycles were safe. But she was able to put it out of her mind when Paul invited her to look at yet another new trade he was testing with Stan.

After spending time discussing FOREX with Paul and Stan, Laura and Ryan headed off to their hotel for the night.

CHAPTER 7

WHEN LAURA AND RYAN GOT home from their trip this time, Laura swore to herself that she would put as much energy into trading as she could. She spent many hours on the phone with Paul and the Grimms in the early morning trading before work. After several months, Laura decided that she still wasn't able to make a profit and began to grow concerned. She mentioned it to Paul, who told her he had just started trading with another Fx company in addition to trading with Stan, and he was seeing profit for the first time that was stable. He had been frustrated too; the losses from some of his trades had wiped out months of hard work. Laura decided to join this new company, called Fx Futuristics, and began trading live in the morning at five o'clock, which was a better time for her. She felt bad about missing Stan's webinars but was glad she could still look at his numbers every night. She also felt comforted by the fact that her robot account with him was also rising more quickly now. She had about half a million dollars when she last asked Stan her balance. She and Ryan were hoping to be able to take out some money once they were ready to move and buy a new house. They wanted to move back to the East Coast, closer to Laura's mom. They also got a call from their friends Jan and Josh, who had decided to borrow money from a home equity line of credit in order to invest. Josh was going to look into how much he could borrow. Laura assured him that all was well with the fund.

After three and a half months of trading with Fx Futuristics, Laura decided that although she was becoming more profitable, she was having a hard time getting enough sleep. She decided to take a few days off and invited her mom, Mary, to come to visit for a long weekend. Mary decided to fly into Chico the following week. Since Mary didn't have the money to pay for a flight, Laura took care of the arrangements. Laura picked her up at the airport early the next Friday morning. Laura was excited for her mom to visit, since she had never been to Chico before.

Laura greeted her mom with a kiss on the cheek and a hug.

"Laura, it's good to finally get here!" Mary said. Laura and Mary talked nonstop all the way to Laura's house. Ryan and Laura took her to the lake and took her out on their boat. Mary enjoyed the scenery, as it was breathtaking. As they traveled over the water, they spotted a blue heron nesting in a tall tree. Then they spotted an eagle flying overhead. The sun was out, and it was a beautiful day. The pine trees were dense green giants that lined the mountains in the distance. Many other people were out enjoying the day as well. They waved at a young wake boarder as he glided over the crest of the waves, like the pendulum of a clock in perfect tempo. When they got back to the shore, they loaded up the boat at the dock and drove back to the house.

"That was so beautiful. I can't believe I saw that eagle soaring overhead!" Mary exclaimed excitedly.

"I know, Mom. We love going out to the lake. I'm glad you could join us," Laura replied.

Laura sat down on the couch with Mary and began to share some of the details of her trading. She told her mom about Stan and Stan's father, the evangelist. She even pulled up some webinars of Stan so her mom could see what he was like. She also showed a book to Mary that Stan's father, Fred, had written on faith. The phone rang while they were sitting on the couch. It was Paul.

"Sorry, Mom, I'm going to take this call. It should just be a minute," Laura said. Her mom nodded.

"Hello?" Laura said as she got up and went to the back door. She opened the door and started to walk out to the patio to a lounge chair.

"Are you ready for some bad news? Are you sitting down?" Paul asked in an ominous tone.

"No and no … but tell me anyway," she responded, not knowing what to expect.

"Stan's dead. He was killed in a motorcycle accident today. I just spoke with some of the EMTs at the scene," Paul said, with a sigh and a heavy breath.

"What? It can't be. I can't even believe that," Laura gasped.

"I can't believe it either. I just can't *be..be..believe* it," he said, his voice dissolving into a soft cry.

"I don't know what to say," Laura said with a heavy heart. Questions started bombarding her mind about the funds she had invested and Stan's poor family … he was such a great person. It was too much for her to think about all at once. She was almost overwhelmed to the point of shutting down emotionally. She became numb.

After a few moments of silence, Paul said, "I'm going to go… and make some more calls."

"Thanks, Paul. Uh … I'll talk to you soon," Laura replied as her brain began to sense that someone was speaking to her, and she needed to respond. She hung up the phone, still in shock. Then she went back inside to let her mom know.

"You mean the man who we were just watching videos of?" Mary asked.

"Yes, I mean, I can't even believe it, but yes," Laura muttered.

The dogs started to bark. *Ryan must be home. He's really not going to believe this,* she thought. They had discussed this unlikely scenario before, about asking Stan what his plan was if something happened to him. But Laura never said anything to Stan. She thought it might not be an appropriate question. She went outside to meet Ryan, who was still in his car with the window rolled down. She couldn't hold back the tears anymore and said to Ryan, her eyes filled with tears, "Stan's dead. He died in a motorcycle accident today."

Ryan's face got very serious, and he got out of the car and slammed the door shut. He walked over toward the trees near the side of the driveway and sat on a rock. "I can't believe that. We always said we should talk to him about what would happen with the funds if something happens to him." Ryan was very upset. It all seemed like a bad dream. They sat there together in silence for a few minutes. They decided it would be best to call Paul back later and talk with him more, once they had some time to digest this terrible news more fully. They both couldn't help but think about what was going to happen with the fund and their investment. Laura felt bad about thinking about that now but knew that it was going to have to be addressed sooner or later.

They went back inside and sat down on the couch with Mary. No one said anything for a few minutes. Mary said she was going to take a nap and leave them alone to talk. She felt it was better to give them some space. In the silence, after what seemed like hours but was only less than one, Laura decided to call Paul back for more information.

"I was just wondering if you had heard anything else about the accident or what the plan is with the funeral?" she asked Paul.

"Yes, they are going to have a memorial service next Wednesday. I was told that Stan was hit by an eighteen-wheeler. He was riding his son's Yamaha motorcycle, and it had been having some mechanical trouble. Debbie said he was taking it out to see if he could figure out what was wrong with it. Apparently, he lost control and hit the eighteen-wheeler head-on, and both of his legs were somehow torn off on impact ..." Paul's voice drifted off, and he got quiet.

"Wow, I don't even know what to say, Paul. Please let me know when you find out the details of the memorial service. Ryan and I would like to come to show our support," she said.

Laura remembered that Josh and Jan were going to borrow money to put into the robot fund, and she decided to call them. Josh answered the phone.

"Laura, it's funny you called just now," Josh said. "I'm going in to sign the paperwork for the home equity line today."

"Well, that's why I'm calling. Stan is dead; he died in a motorcycle accident today."

"Wow, really? The one with the fund?" Josh asked.

"The one and only. It's interesting timing, isn't it, Josh?" Laura said.

"It sure is. I'm sorry to hear about that," he said.

"I'm sorry too," she replied.

CHAPTER 8

Are not all angels ministering spirits sent to
serve those who will inherit salvation?
—Hebrews 1:14

IN THE SUPERNATURAL REALM, LINED up at the entrance of the Grand
Gate Hall, twelve large gold horns played by twelve of the most highly
gifted angelic musicians of heaven produced sound waves that created the
typical entrance song for the head angel of protection, Dunamis. All angels
stood at attention, as Dunamis, who was given high regard as God's chief
of the guardian angels, made his entrance. If one could slow them down
long enough (as they traveled at the speed of light on earth), they would see
these angelical beings hovering over them at approximately sixteen feet tall
and floating in the air in their bright white and gold crepe paper-textured
robes. Over their robes were thick gold metal sheets of armor surrounding
their chests. They had two arms and two legs that were as thick as large tree
trunks. Their faces were glowing light, and they had two large greenish-
blue eyes that created beams of light like flashlights, one on each side of
their faces. They had no nose but had a large mouth below their eyes and
two large rows of white pearls for teeth. Their hair was a distinctive feature
for them. It was composed of actual light waves, ranging from red light to
violet, and it extended sixteen feet behind them and acted as propellers,
or wings, capable of shooting them through the supernatural world to the
earth faster than the blink of an eye.

As a subdivision of the mansion and expansive courtyard of the Guardian
and Warring Angel Strategic Planning Zone, Grand Gate Hall was one of
the most beautifully adorned rooms. There was a gold staircase with smooth
jade banisters, approximately one foot wide, on either side of it that spiraled

from the top of the tenth tier all the way down to a large seating area on the ground level, with over ten thousand seats made of finely carved olive wood. At the front of the room there was a pearl stairway ascending to a platform that showcased the throne of honor, which was composed of smooth platinum and studded with large purple diamonds and was suspended by four long braided silk purple ropes. Above, there was no ceiling. There was bright, heavenly blue sky as far as the eye could see and beams of glorious light shining down into the room that were reflected by the intricately woven gold, silver, and bronze flooring toward the lower portion of the walls, which set the room aglow with a unique shimmering brilliance.

The meeting today was called by Dunamis; it wasn't on the weekly schedule. But certain issues had arisen that required immediate attention. Dunamis and several of his troops has just returned from a recent skirmish in the northwest portion of the United States. His armor had indentations on the chest plate that were the size of cannonballs, and the lower portion of his robe was dripping with strands of blackish-green gooey mucous. He had a large gash on his left shoulder that most likely coincided with the sharp edge of a demonic weapon. His lieutenant Arnamis was not consulted in advance about this meeting, and hearing of it only ten minutes prior had caused him immense concern, although he was thankful that Dunamis was safe. Over the past several months Dunamis and Arnamis had been following a certain situation in Olympia, Washington, that had seemed to be escalating. At the sight of Dunamis, Arnamis wondered if their worst-case scenario had finally come to pass. After the song ended, there was silence.

After saluting the angels, Dunamis took his place and settled into the golden chair. The anticipation grew as the angels waited for him to speak.

"As all of you are aware, I have been observing Mr. Stan Powers of Olympia, Washington, for quite some time. I would like to review his case today for those of you who do not know him. When Stan was thirteen years old, God assigned me to him as his guardian to protect him and watch over him. Shortly after being assigned to him, I began to see an increased number of attacks on Stan's mind and also on his family member's minds by demons Asm and Chaos. Over the past several years, I have witnessed mentally anguishing attacks on Stan by Grinoir, the demon of cruelty; and an almost fatal accident caused by Haden, the demon of war and fear. Arnamis and I have personally fought against these demons on more than one occasion. However, what concerned me the most over the past several weeks was the demonic influence of Solum, the spirit of depression, pervading Stan's soul. In fact, I have just returned from a battle with Solum. As you can see from my appearance, it was a rough battle."

Dunamis paused as one of the assistants floated up to him and gave him a refreshing drink of honey nectar. Dunamis was grateful for this act of respect and kindness. It gave him a renewed energy to finish his difficult but necessary update. He knew they had just suffered a devastating blow that was the result of a methodically delivered scheme, maddeningly employed over the years by the cruel wicked ones of the 33rd Battalion. Dunamis was preparing the words in his mind to convey this sentiment. By now, most of the angels had realized that the curiosity about the humans and why God had created them would still remain a mystery in their collective minds; they knew they were responsible for these creatures regardless, and they had all made it their top priority to protect them until Jesus returned to earth.

"Unfortunately ... I must report that I was not able to protect Stan from Solum in this last battle, and Stan is now deceased." Murmurs arose around the room, and many angels began to raise their arms to ask a question. Anticipating the curiosity, Dunamis added, "Before anyone asks, I must say that I currently do not know the location of his soul." Arms went down around the room. "We have a situation that requires the utmost wisdom and endurance to address and could involve the extrication of hundreds of souls.

"So what do we do now?" one of the guardian angels asked from the back of the room. "How can we be of service?"

"I'm glad you asked," said Dunamis. "We have a long list of people whose souls will be in need of defending and, ultimately, liberating when they find out the news about Stan. Unfortunately, there is more to this situation than meets the eye. This is going to be a long, difficult assignment, perhaps the most formidable we have had to date, and I'm asking for volunteers."

It took only seconds for every angel in the room to stand at attention again to signify their acceptance of the mission. The angels were ready to act when the people started to pray.

CHAPTER *9*

On the Tuesday following Stan's tragic death, Laura and Ryan embarked on their long drive to Olympia, Washington. They couldn't help but remember how joyous their last adventure had been, even though the weather had been treacherous. This time, though, they were dreading the trip. Many other traders and their families from across the country also made travel arrangements to be at Stan's memorial service, which was to be at 1:00 p.m. on Wednesday at the Rock Church. Laura knew that her friend Paul would be there but was unsure what to expect or what to say to Stan's family. She was overwhelmed with grief and couldn't imagine what they were feeling, especially his poor wife, Debbie. She knew Debbie was going to speak at the service, according to Paul, which in Laura's mind took a lot of courage.

When Laura and Ryan arrived in Olympia they decided to drive to the location where the accident had occurred. They were able to see a ten-foot-long skid mark that veered off the road. They assumed that was the location of the accident. They felt a sense of sadness overwhelm them as they thought of Stan's suffering. Other than that mark, there was no other indication of the horrific event that had occurred a few days earlier. They sat in their car and prayed for Stan's family before heading to their hotel.

The following day, Laura, dressed in her black silk wrap dress and black sandals, and Ryan, in his black linen pants and dark gray button-down short-sleeved shirt arrived thirty minutes early to Rock Church. They were shocked to see an over-flowing parking lot. They were not able to find a parking space and parked across the street. As they walked up to the church holding hands, there were two highway patrol officers at the entrance of the church under the portico. Laura couldn't tell if they were on duty or just friends of Stan's, paying their respects. Inside, there must have been over two thousand people filling the pews, including the balcony. Laura was not in the mood to have a conversation and only waved to Paul and his wife from her seat in the third row. She knew she would be able to speak to him afterward. After what seemed like only a few minutes, a worship band began to play what they would learn was one of Stan's favorite songs, "Healing Rain" by Michael W. Smith. In the background, pictures of Stan were projected up on the screen of his early life, from traveling with his family in the band, all the way to his wedding, birth of his sons, and a ceremony of a renewal of Debbie and Stan's wedding vows from the previous year. One couldn't help but smile at some of the pictures of Stan, especially of him with his mullet haircut, donning bell-bottom pants and matching psychedelic shirt. A second song started, and Laura realized it was the "Hey, Hey, We're the Monkees" song, which made many people laugh out loud, as no one expected that random silly song at a memorial service. *But then again, this is for Stan. He was like no other,* Laura thought. *It's the perfect song.* For most onlookers, though, their smiles faded as they remembered why they were there.

After the song, Debbie stood up to speak. The room was silent. Debbie had a crumpled tissue and a piece of paper in her left hand and still managed to grasp the mike stand with it, while using her right hand to adjust the microphone. It appeared as if she had been crying, as was expected. But she seemed resolute and determined to speak to the crowd of people looking to her for comforting words. To Debbie, it seemed as if the sea of faces was speaking to her: *Please, say something to erase the pain. Tell us this isn't real … It's just a bad dream … You can wake up now.* For a second she felt ill. Her head was swimming. She took a minute, grabbed the podium, focused her gaze to her handwritten notes, took a deep breath in the silent room, and, with a steady voice, proclaimed,

"Hello, everyone. I'm glad you could be here with me today. This is a celebration of Stan's life. Please join with me in the celebration. I want to tell everyone what an awesome man Stan was. He was an awesome father, an awesome friend, and an awesome husband. I couldn't be more thankful for the years we had together. Every minute with Stan was a gift from God." Debbie took a moment, looked down toward the podium, fought back against the tightening grip on her throat, and then brought her head back up. She continued. "Stan gave me two wonderful sons, Jason and Jack, who are here today as well. I'd like to speak for them. They love their dad. They will miss him greatly, but they know he will always be with them. Stan always put God first and then us. They are the awesome men they are today because of Stan." At that point, Debbie cleared her throat and again thanked the people for coming before leaving the stage to sit between her sons in the first row.

After several of Stan's lifelong friends spoke to the crowd, the pastor, Leonard Green, slowly rose from his seat and walked up to the microphone. He was a stocky middle-aged man with a pleasant face and short curly gray hair. After quietly clearing his throat, he spoke.

"I want to say how dear a friend Stan was to me personally. We played golf on many occasions. Stan actually invited me to Hawaii to play golf. He was one of a kind. I'll never forget the way he communicated with one person at the airport. He wanted to sit in the airport bar. I know that sounds strange, but he invited himself to sit down with an older gentleman at a table by himself. Next thing you know, he was smoking a cigarette with the man and leading him to Christ. It's funny, because Stan did not smoke, but he was willing to do what he could to relate to others."

People laughed at this story and the image of Stan smoking a cigarette and having a conversation in a bar.

"I want to use the word *eagle* to describe Stan because I visualize eagles as powerful creatures that are natural leaders, and that's how I saw Stan. Each letter in eagle stands for an attribute that Stan demonstrated to his fellow brothers and sisters. First off, there is the E. He was energized. I like to call him the Energizer. I don't know if he ever slept." Many people in the crowd were nodding in agreement and smiling. "Second, the A stands for *a* good man. I know that's cheating a little bit, but he really was a good man. He would give you the shirt off his back. Next, the G stands for godly. Stan was a member of this church for many years and served on this very same worship band until last week. He was a friend in times of trouble. He did unto others as he would have had them do unto him. The L stands for loveable and loyal. He was both. You could count on Stan to be by your side and not be judgmental. And last, the second E stands for endurance. He was a man of God and, like Paul in Philippians 3:14, was one 'to press on toward the mark for the prize of the high calling of God in Christ Jesus … to which he has now received.' Let us pray." Pastor Leonard did an impressive job of staying composed throughout the prayer. It was only as he said amen" that his voice seemed to break.

After the service, Laura and Ryan went into the lobby to talk to Paul. Laura was feeling a little bit better. The words of the pastor had been encouraging—*another E word that describes Stan,* she thought. She saw Stan's mom and dad in the lobby briefly, and as she went by she could see that Fred was definitely in a somber mood, compared to his persona the day she saw him at Stan's sister's house. And his mother was not able to keep her composure but dissolved into tears and went back into the sanctuary. Laura had thought that Stan's dad would say some words at the service and was slightly surprised that he did not. His sister, Bethany, and brother, Nolan, were talking to one person after another and hugging them as they gave their condolences.

While Ryan slipped away to use the restroom, Laura found Paul and went up to him. He looked to have been in a deep conversation with a couple of other traders that Laura recognized. As she walked up to the group, the traders abruptly lowered their voices, and the conversation came to a halt. Laura, ignoring the blank stares by the other traders, gave Paul a hug. He mentioned that Stan's lawyers were supposed to be in touch with Debbie in the next week to discuss how to make arrangements for people to get their money out of the fund Stan set up. Laura felt uncomfortable asking any questions about the fund because she didn't want to come across as being insensitive. She let the matter drop for the moment and gave Paul another hug; then they said their good-byes. There were a lot of people there she did not know, and after a few minutes of talking and giving their condolences to Stan's parents, sister, and brother, Laura and Ryan left the church.

CHAPTER *10*

Watch out for false prophets. They come to you in
sheep's clothing, but inwardly they are ferocious wolves
—Matthew 7:15

ONE WEEK AFTER THE MEMORIAL service Laura was walking into Pier One when her cell phone rang. It was Paul. "Hi, Laura, can you talk?" he asked. She hadn't heard from Paul since the service and was anxious to get some news about her funds.

"Yes. How are you?" she replied.

"Not so good, Laura … it was all a lie … a fake … there is no money. Stan had nothing but what he took from all of us. There are no lawyers. It's all a sham. I heard that he never made money trading FOREX."

Laura couldn't believe her ears. She started to get tunnel vision standing there by a shelf of cobalt blue wine glasses in the front of the store. All of a sudden, shopping was the last thing she wanted to do.

"What do you mean, Paul? How could that be? So many traders traded with him, and you were with him, trading at his house all the time. You saw his trade accounts and balances," Laura said with disbelief in her voice. "I mean, didn't you know people who had done the Birth of a Million? Stan said he had people that were doing it." Her mind was bombarded with thoughts, and she tried to focus on Paul's response.

"I never met anyone. As far as Stan's accounts go, they must have all been practice accounts. I found out one of the church members had gone to his house the morning of the accident to demand his money from Stan. He was tired of Stan giving him the runaround, so he said if Stan didn't get his money, he would tell the pastor of the church. So Stan agreed to go to the bank that morning to get the money." He paused for a minute and then continued. "I think he planned to kill himself because he knew he couldn't pay them, and everyone was about to find out he was a fraud."

Laura didn't know what to say or think. She kept waiting to hear Paul say he was just kidding, but that didn't happen.

"Paul, please tell me this isn't happening!" she yelled out, and quickly realized she needed to keep her voice down. She took a deep breath, rested her elbow on the nearest shelf of scented pillar candles, and put her hand to her forehead, hoping no one had heard her outburst.

"Hang in there, Laura. I'm going to keep digging for information. I'll be talking to the pastor tomorrow. Maybe Stan did make some money and hid it somewhere in a blind trust or something. I don't know if the robot account exists or not. Maybe his lawyers stole all the money from him. I don't know. There are a lot of questions right now. My friend Shane put his parents' retirement, half a million dollars, into his robot account. I know I have about three hundred thousand dollars in there, including my grandson's money."

Laura told Paul about her investment as well. After a few minutes, she said good-bye, wishing this was just a bad dream. As she walked out of the store, she thought about how she was going to tell Ryan the news. She knew the sooner she told him, the better, but she thought it would be better to tell him in person.

When Laura got home she had a few hours before Ryan was expected. She decided to watch the memorial service for Stan online, as his family had it posted for those who couldn't make it to his service. She watched Debbie to study her demeanor. She certainly seemed grief-stricken, but did she know something? There were a lot of questions. She got on the PowersFx Facebook page and saw that so many people were leaving messages for the family and sharing their stories about Stan. There was one man in particular who seemed to take Stan's death particularly poorly. His name was Terry. He kept saying how much he loved Stan and stated over and over again that he was his best friend and was not able to sleep and didn't know if he'd ever get over this. To Laura, Terry's words seemed a little strange, but she figured that everyone grieved in his own way.

When Ryan got home, she told him the bad news. He took it better than she thought he would. But there were so many questions. They truly felt that there had to be a sane explanation. Laura felt like this whole thing was her fault, from starting to trade FOREX to wanting to invest money with Stan. She was thankful that Ryan didn't blame her. There wasn't much they could do, other than wait for an update from Paul. They decided to start planning for their future, as they were essentially starting over again financially. Laura decided to hold off on trading until she got more answers. For now, Stan's brother, Nolan, was taking over the trading sessions for PowersFx. Laura personally did not think it would be the same without Stan.

One Week Later

Laura's phone rang. It was Paul.

"Hey, Laura, do you want to hear something crazy?"

Laura sighed. Almost every call from Paul lately started in this fashion, and it was something she wanted to squelch before it became routine; although deep down she knew she had absolutely no control of that. Only hoping for the best, she said, "Sure."

"I was at Stan's early this morning, talking with Debbie and the boys, trying to help them figure out what was going on with Stan's trading accounts. The FBI came bursting in the front door and ordered everyone to go out front onto the lawn. They made us lie down on our stomachs with hands above our heads, and then they frisked us. I swear, my heart was racing so hard I began to sweat and had chest pains. I almost ended up in the emergency room, but they finally let us go inside and sit down. It was surreal."

Laura was shocked. "Wow, Paul, what happened next? What did they say?"

"They didn't talk to us too much at first, but they confiscated his vehicles—the Cobra, the Porsche, and the Lexus, as well as all of the motorcycles—and they had Debbie get all of her jewelry. They even mentioned that they were taking the yacht. I saw the local news van outside, but I didn't want to go out there and get bombarded by reporters. After a while I decided to ask the FBI some questions, just to see if they would tell me anything. I told them I was curious about his trading accounts. Honestly, Laura, it sounds like they had been watching him for a while. Somehow, someone brought him to their attention. I'm not sure … but they did tell me that he wasn't a successful trader and had no money in his trading account. Then they started asking me questions about my relationship with Stan. I told them I'd tell them anything I could. I got one of the agent's business cards. His name is Peter Hawkins. He said I could call anytime I wanted to get an update, and if he could tell me anything he would. You know, Laura, I was thinking about it, and I remember now a couple of times when Debbie came into the study to tell Stan that there wasn't any money in the account for groceries. At the time, I didn't think anything of it, but now I am wondering if it really was that obvious, and I just missed it."

"I'm sitting here in shock, Paul. I can't believe the FBI raided you guys. This situation is incredible. Who knows what was really going on. You know, I may want that agent's number, just in case. I guess I'll get on the Internet and see what the local news has to say."

The local Olympia news already had an article about Stan in their evening edition of the paper. The internet headline read, "FBI raids house of the late Stan Powers." It went on to mention the confiscation of his vehicles and motorcycles and showed a video clip of them being loaded on trailers and removed from his house. Laura was starting to feel sick to her stomach. She had this sinking feeling that anything they'd invested with Stan they most likely would never see again. She started to think about her legal options.

The next day, Laura called Paul. " I'm very concerned about all of this," she told him. "I don't see this ending well for all of us. Have you thought about getting a lawyer?"

"Yes, there is a large group of us going in together to see if we can recover anything from the sale of his possessions. But probably not likely; there were apparently over three hundred people who invested with Stan, and about thirty million dollars is unaccounted for."

"Oh my goodness! That is so terrible," she said and then added cynically, "I hope some money can be repaid, but I bet most of the money will go to lawyer fees. Like, who cares about the victims?"

"Stan had a life insurance policy for about one hundred thousand dollars, but I don't think anyone can touch that."

"Wow, that seems so miniscule compared to what we all thought he was worth; it seems pathetic." As an afterthought, she asked, "Oh, by the way, Paul, do you know a guy named Terry? I've seen him on the Facebook page for Stan. He said he was Stan's best friend."

"Oh, that's his neighbor. Apparently, he had Stan's Porsche and said that Stan gave it to him for collateral. But the boys say Stan just parked it at his house because he didn't have any room in his garage. Now Terry is starting a campaign against Stan online. He texted Debbie and told her he hopes Stan rots deep below the earth for eternity. People are starting to get pretty angry with each other online, arguing with one another and being vicious about it, I might add. Sadly, there is a lot of conjecture on his death too, whether it was accidental or a suicide…but I know what I believe."

"This is becoming almost ludicrous. I hope we get some more answers soon."

"Me too. Laura. Have a good night."

The following day, Laura and Ryan were discussing Stan.

"I just can't understand what happened. How could anyone take money like that from someone? Something must have really gone wrong for him. People really trusted him. It was like taking candy from a baby," Laura said.

"Yeah, and then abandoning the baby on someone's doorstep," Ryan added.

As Laura was about to respond, Cal called. Laura put him on speaker phone. "Cal, I guess you heard about the FBI raid as well? I was just telling Ryan that what Stan did was worse than taking candy from a baby. And then he added it was like taking candy from a baby and then abandoning the baby on someone's doorstep," Laura repeated to Cal.

Not wanting to let go of the neglected baby analogy, Cal added, "Yeah, and the baby had a dirty diaper."

"And a bill for delivering the baby was pinned to his diaper," Ryan added with controlled sarcasm. They all laughed at the absurdity of it.

"This could go on forever," Laura said of the sad but true analogy.

"Anyway, Laura, I was just calling to see how you guys were doing," Cal said. He hadn't had the money to invest in Stan's robot account when the opportunity arose. Now, what was considered a disadvantage at the time turned out to be a blessing in disguise.

"We're doing okay, Cal. I think our money is long gone, though."

"Well, keep me posted. I'll be praying for you guys."

"Thanks Cal, the more prayers, the better."

CHAPTER 11

Be alert and of sober mind. Your enemy
the devil prowls around like a roaring lion
looking for someone to devour.
—1 Peter 5:8

MANY YEARS HAD GONE BY on earth since his first assignment began, and Wink was sitting in his dusty, hot, molten-rock study, reflecting over his journey. He now slithered along at fourteen foot six and was second in command, directly under Ashkran, of the 33rd Battalion of the northwest portion of the US. He was quite proud of his accomplishments, working to haunt Stan Powers's soul. Asm and Chaos had been instrumental in waging warfare on Stan's will, causing him to desire to obtain wealth for himself. If you asked Asm, he would say, with his feigned humility, that it was not a hard task, as most children of God are selfish by nature. But in actuality, Stan surprised even him by his generosity to his fellow man. Stan did have good character, and it had been a struggle to plant the right temptations in his path.

The turning point was actually a stroke of luck for Asm; it was one of those things that Asm couldn't even have planned. When Stan was in his twenties and was living in Olympia, he had a flat tire one day in front of the local casino. Asm planted a thought in his head that he needed to go inside for a soda because he was thirsty. When Stan did go inside, Asm whispered motivating thoughts to an attractive waitress to get her to walk in Stan's vicinity and offering him a free drink. Stan took the drink and decided that playing a little blackjack wouldn't hurt. He knew how to play very well, growing up on the bus, where he often played with his siblings.

Chaos manipulated the deck so that Stan was able to win. He had a long winning streak that night and made ten thousand dollars. The demons knew they had Stan right where they wanted him. Stan became a regular at the casino and also began drinking quite heavily. He became well known at the casino for his amazing winning streak, and the regulars at the casino referred to him as the Shark. He was winning tens of thousands of dollars each night. One night, after Debbie, who was his girlfriend at that time, confronted Stan about the tremendous amount of time he spent gambling, Stan stormed off to the casino to get his mind off things. On this particular night, he became especially bold with his betting. The demons decided it was time to strike. Stan's lucky streak ended that night. He started losing and never stopped. The casino lent money to Stan over and above his ability to pay it back. He ended up losing his beautiful new red Ferrari that he had just purchased a month earlier and also lost his brand-new Harley.

Stan finally decided to quit gambling, mostly because he was out of money and the casino barred him from returning, and he decided to work for Amway. He swore to himself that he would never put himself in a position to lose again. The demons were excited to see Stan make that vow and planned for more attacks on Stan. As they knew, these types of vows could quickly turn into strongholds in the minds of the children of God. And strongholds were the ultimate traps perpetrated by the demons during spiritual warfare. Appearing as black webbing that formed long tendrils around a human's soul, the angels sought to destroy these strongholds by piercing them with the sword of the Lord, the written Word. They encouraged Stan by the renewing of his mind by giving him thoughts that coincided with God's Word as to his value as God's child, and they showed him the power of his thoughts and words. Stan knew the importance of his thoughts and seemed to do a good job telling others likewise, but over time, he wondered whether things would ever change for him.

Debbie and Stan got married a year after he quit gambling and drinking, after what Debbie referred to as Stan's "temporary suspension of reality". She had always had faith that Stan would come to his senses and was content that he'd quit gambling before more damage was done to their relationship. She wanted to have a nice life with Stan, a beautiful house, and beautiful clothing to wear. She had contradictory desires. At times, she wished he was still making the kind of money he made when he gambled, but at the same time, she hoped he would start to be the man of

God his father was. She believed Fred Powers when he talked about God wanting to bless his children. She thought that since having nice things was important to her, then God would want her to have them.

Accolades had to be given to Asm, who had been whispering thoughts into her mind consistently about how she deserved to have nice things. So shortly after their marriage, she got her first credit card, which was fun for Debbie, who never held a full-time job in her life. She had no experience with credit scores, nor did she care about finding the card with the best interest rate. She felt having a credit card or two would be a great way to buy some of the beautiful furniture and clothing she wanted. She asked Stan to get a couple of credit cards as well, as she made the argument that she could get better deals and discounts at her favorite stores if she had a credit card for each of them.

Unfortunately, Stan's Amway career was not able to support the kind of debt that Debbie was so recklessly creating. *I can only sell so many gallons of carpet cleaner a month*, he had thought. Debbie seemed heartbroken. He didn't want to argue with Debbie, so he started looking into real estate. After several meetings with friends, he was able to convince several of his friends to go into purchasing property with him. But it seemed as if the progress was very slow, and Debbie's spending was only accelerating.

On the way home from church one day, Stan and Debbie were driving in their 1992 Blue Honda Civic, and the brakes failed, thanks to Grinoir and Haden repeatedly distracting Stan every time he thought about taking the car into the shop due to squeaky brakes. They had just started descending a long, winding road when Stan put his foot to the brake pedal and pushed. To his dismay, they continued to race down the hill, gaining momentum by the second. He finally swerved into the guard rail at the bottom of the hill, right before they would have plowed into a large white boulder beyond the rail by ten yards. They both walked away with limited injuries; Stan broke his left collarbone, and Debbie managed to have only abrasions on her neck and chest where the seatbelt had dug into her skin to keep her from hitting the windshield.

Stan was getting angry with God. He knew this wasn't how his life was supposed to be. In the heavenly realm, the angels Dunamis and Aramis were shaking their heads, wondering why he wasn't thankful to have escaped that catastrophe with only limited injuries. They did their best at that last minute to veer his car into the guard rail. If they hadn't been held up by Chaos in battle, they would have been able to stop the entire event from occurring, but Stan's lack of faith wasn't helping them gain any victories.

One day, Nolan called him to discuss trying something new called FOREX. Stan was immediately interested. He really didn't think he had any other options. So Stan started to read all of the material he could on FOREX. He was blessed with a photographic memory, so he was able to assimilate and retain a lot of information very quickly. After months of practicing, Stan opened a trading account. He was doing very well at trading, and his brother noticed right away.

"Stan, how much money did you make so far this month?" Nolan asked with extreme curiosity.

"Well, Nolan, I believe I tripled my money, so *only* two thousand dollars," Stan replied, smiling from ear to ear.

"Do you think you can keep it up?"

"Sure, I've been working on some trading strategies, and the back testing looks great, so now I'm going to forward test a few more. Get ready to make some money, big brother," Stan exclaimed.

"Would you please trade for me, Stan?" Nolan asked, smiling widely.

"Sure, but if I lose … never mind … I'm not going to lose. I really think this is what I'm supposed to do," Stan said.

Over the next two years Stan did very well for himself, making over a hundred thousand dollars in his first six months and then doubling that two times over the remaining eighteen months. He created several other practice accounts to work out his new trading strategies. He and Nolan started his trading company to have other traders sign up to learn to trade from Stan. There was a lot of interest in Stan's company; he had a lot of friends. Within three months of starting his business, he came across a company that sold robots, or automated trading strategies, that could be placed on his account and would initiate a trade based on certain preprogrammed signals. The company from which he finally decided to purchase the robot guaranteed a consistent rate of return for the trader, if used properly. At the time, Stan neglected to realize there were so many ways to use it *improperly*. After two months, the robot account, which had been doing phenomenally, margined out, costing Stan over one hundred thousand dollars.

When Stan woke up that morning and saw that he had lost so much money, he panicked. He looked at the robot trade to see what had happened and realized that there was a report that had come out overnight, which just barely triggered the robot to do a sell trade of the euro, only for the value of the euro to start rising after the report came out. *Well, I better remember to turn this thing off overnight if I'm not going to watch it,* he thought. Stan just knew he would continue to be profitable with the robot. He realized that he needed to get more funds into the robot account and had an idea. Rather than taking any funds out of his other accounts, he would get other people to put money into the account to make the amount grow quicker and replace what he had lost. Thus, the robot fund was created.

Over time, Stan's robot account became quite popular. Word got out about Stan's investment account, and people began to inquire about it. He was investing money for family and friends and making a good profit on it as well. Even at his Boot Camp, Stan was able to find new people to whom he could offer the robot fund as a safe investment until they could trade well on their own. But unfortunately, there were more losing streaks to come.

With the volatility of the markets, Stan started to lose on a regular basis. He didn't think it was a sin to let people think he was still trading successfully, though. He knew things would turn around eventually. However, almost overnight, his normal trading strategies weren't working like they used to work. Stan knew he had to do something, and he started to look for new investments other than FOREX once again. In the meantime, he had a string of people asking to get their money out of his robot fund at the same time. It was an unfortunate coincidence for Stan, he believed, but in reality, it was due to Grinoir's repeatedly whispered suggestions that their money wasn't safe that led them to want to take it out.

Solum was instrumental in Stan's downfall by whispering *You're doomed* into Stan's mind and giving him migraine headaches. Stan was having a hard time focusing and was getting to the point where he didn't want to do his nightly webinars. However, he was able to hide his anxiety and pain from the migraines. He was a firm believer in maintaining mental control and never going emotional, which is a skill he had been perfecting throughout his trading career. People continued to look forward to Stan's webinars, and he continued to get daily e-mails, asking him what their current account balances were in the robot fund. Stan had a sense of growing desperation like he had never known before. And his anger at God came back with a vengeance, no matter how hard he struggled to stifle it.

CHAPTER *12*

And no wonder, for Satan himself masquerades as
an angel of light. It is not surprising, then, if his
servants also masquerade as servants of righteousness.
Their end will be what their actions deserve.
—2 Corinthians 11:14–15

IT WASN'T VERY LONG AFTER the FBI raid that the online chatter over Stan reached significant proportions. Terry, Stan's so-called best friend, decided to start a new website called Bewarethebamboozlers.com, basically created to allow people to complain about what wrongs had been done to them, either by Stan Powers or any other scammer. Grinoir was especially proud of giving Terry that idea. He could watch the back-and-forth insults for hours, with amusement at how the children of God acted when things didn't go their way. The lost-soul count was rising quickly. Through supernatural eyes, there was a fog of flies blanketing the individuals involved in the dispute. They had formed from the maggots that were birthed from the decaying of their souls.

Laura had been doing a search online to find the latest information about Stan when she came across the website. She thought it might be helpful to learn more information. She realized there was a certain segment of the people who had known Stan and his family for years, who could not be convinced that Stan would ever take money from people or, worse yet, commit suicide to escape justice. They were adamant that he would never leave Debbie in that fashion. On the other hand, there was the group of people who had been Stan's victims and were consequently seething with rage. Each side seemed to have a spokesperson, neither of whom was interested in hearing the other side, only proving they were right.

"Of course you think he's innocent of wrongdoing, you stupid idiot. You didn't lose three hundred thousand dollars!" said one man, whose username was Furiousandbroke.

"Why would Stan do that? He helped so many people. I know a friend to whom Stan gave five thousand dollars to pay medical bills," replied Stunnedandsaddened.

"Because Stan was a piece of garbage and a liar … and so are you."

"You better watch it, buddy, or I'll find you and give you something to be furious about!" retaliated Stunnedandsaddened, who was now, in Laura's opinion, more "Provokedandangry." Like a bad car accident, Laura couldn't take her eyes off the screen, even if she'd wanted to.

"You know, I heard Stan was a big gambler over there in Olympia at that casino by the Rock Church."

"He probably went there after church on Sunday," someone typed anonymously.

"That's ridiculous. Stan wasn't a gambler," a Stan supporter retorted.

"I know for a fact that he was; his brother, Nolan, told me so!" Anonymous replied matter-of- factly.

Laura was hoping maybe someone knew something about Stan and could provide new information, but now she was feeling very uneasy on the inside. She was angry too, and Stunnedandsaddened just seemed clueless. *But what if he is right?* It didn't make sense to her that there were so many people typing that Stan had helped them financially in the past. *No, WE helped so many people financially,* she thought. *Stan used our money to do it. I wonder if I paid for Debbie's nice wardrobe.* Finally, she was able to gain control of her thoughts, and she shut off the computer with a long, quiet sigh.

Later that day, Paul called Laura to give her an update and let her know someone had sent him a death threat. He reported the threat to the FBI, but he did hesitate to do so, fearing that they might believe he was Stan's partner in crime. It appeared that many people thought Paul was involved because he spent so much time with Stan. He told Laura that he might have to move out of Olympia if things continued to escalate. A lot of people at the Rock Church were now telling the pastor they would leave the church if he didn't stop supporting Fred Powers's ministry. By this time, people had also written anonymous letters to Fred Powers, pressuring him to sell all of his vehicles and his house to help pay back his son's victims.

Two months after Stan's death, it was declared accidental. Laura and Ryan were surprised by this.

"It would be a huge coincidence that Stan so happened to be killed the day that people were demanding their money back from him. It's obvious that he took money from so many people," Ryan said.

"And it's even more of a 'coincidence' that he escaped having to face all of us after taking thirty million dollars and did not have to be held accountable for it," said Laura.

"And what about Debbie and the boys? They had to be in on it ... How in the world could Debbie not have known?" Ryan asked. To make matters more confusing, the FBI declared Stan's behavior to be consistent with a Ponzi scheme.

At least they can save some money on their taxes by writing off the lost money, she thought. *As if that makes a big difference.*

After another month, Paul called Laura to let her know that one of the victims, a good friend of his, had tried to commit suicide and was in the hospital. Laura felt sad for him. She knew losing money was not pleasant by any means, but she couldn't see why someone would want to kill himself over it. Paul decided to stay in Olympia to be close to his friends and family during this time.

"Hey, Paul, while I have you on the phone, have you heard anything about the court case?" Laura asked.

"Yeah, they are supposed to rule on some of the individual investors separately, and our case was put on the back burner, since our lawyer is basically doing this free of charge," Paul said.

"So basically, anyone with the money to sue is going to be able to recover money?"

"Yep, that's usually how it goes."

In the angelic realm, it was clear that some souls were in danger of being lost. Dunamis and Arnamis had responded to the prayers of the victims of the Ponzi scheme, but the demons of the air were numerous and growing greater in numbers by the day. Each individual soul was being defended by his or her own guardian angel. The angels were whispering

God's words of strength and power into their minds on a continuous basis. They were also ministering to them by giving them new thoughts.

"You know what, Laura?" Ryan asked.

"What?"

"Has it ever occurred to you that God is way more concerned with our inner, spiritual circumstances than our outer, physical circumstances?"

"I've actually been thinking something similar to that as well," Laura said.

"Sometimes God allows these types of things to happen to help us grow in faith—call it a test, if you will," Ryan said.

"I guess," she said, not really able to think about anything other than her new problems. She felt that she had to find the solution, since she blamed herself for being such a fool to invest so much money with a perfect stranger. She also couldn't figure out why no one had seen sooner that Stan was a fraud. *Why didn't Paul pick up on the fact that he never seemed to have money in his account, even for groceries?* All of a sudden, she remembered a time a few months ago when Stan called her out of the blue to schedule her private trading session. At the time, she thought nothing of it, but now it seemed significant. Stan had casually asked her if her friends were still thinking about investing with his robot fund. It didn't seem like a big deal, but Laura had said they weren't ready yet. Stan had to get off of the phone quickly after that, never scheduling her trading session. Thinking about all of it now was making her head hurt. *I will never do something so stupid again—never,* she thought.

And the demons laughed at her personal vow as they planned more attacks.

Part
T W O

One Year Later

CHAPTER *13*

You have enemies? Good. That means you've
stood up for something, sometime in your life.
—Winston Churchill

LAURA AND RYAN WERE LIVING in Jupiter, Texas, in a two-story white
house on ten acres of land, about three miles from Laura's new family
medicine office. She had been recruited by a company called Health For
Today, Inc. She had always wanted to come back to Texas; she had gone
to medical school there. As much as she tried to convince herself that this
had been a good decision, especially because she knew she would be able
to pay her brother back with her sign-on bonus, she knew down in her
heart that she had lost her passion for the medical field. There were just so
many new regulations, and with the implementation of new government
"meaningful use" requirements, she was pressured to see more patients
and spend less time with each of them. The company had been gracious
enough, though, paying her an incentive bonus of fifty thousand dollars.
As soon as that check was received, Laura turned around and gave every
single penny of it to her brother. She knew it was the right thing to do,
but it was not easy to watch that much money come and go so quickly.
The Lord giveth and the Lord taketh away, she thought. She was pretty sure
that was in the Bible. *I should Google it*, she thought. Ryan was out in the
garage, working on a friend's car. He had gotten back into auto body repair
since moving to Texas, due to the lack of trees in Central Texas. It was his
second passion, and Laura felt that he had a special gift for it. They lived
about forty-five minutes south of Dallas, but it seemed like they were in
the middle of nowhere. Laura had gotten home from another long day of

work and was remembering her first few weeks in Jupiter and all of the difficulties they had.

Her first thought was that Jupiter was a fitting name, since their experiences so far had been extraterrestrial. On their first day in Texas, they woke up to the sound of shotguns. Evidently, since their house was by the lake at a dead end, people would park at the end of the road and hunt for doves from early in the morning until dusk. During deer hunting season, people would leave behind various deer body parts and deer skins after their successful hunting expeditions. Even the move to Texas was a hassle, with the movers not delivering their belongings until two weeks after they arrived. She was forced to go out shopping for a new wardrobe for work. Usually, she would have jumped at the chance, but the "new and improved" frugal Laura had been trying to save money, and buying new clothes was not a priority in their budget. Then there was the reaction of the patients to her taking over for their beloved retiring Dr. Freeman. They had been less than accepting of her. Some of the patients were very nice, but many were missing their doctor of thirty or so years and felt that their health care was not under their control. They were also concerned about the cost of the new universal health insurance they had to obtain. Unfortunately, Laura's front office staff had to take the brunt of their complaints.

As it related to her front office staff, the Health for Today consultants had helped Laura find her employees. She didn't realize at the time that she would have to deal with an employee who happened to be an alcoholic. Over time, this employee, Daisy, became very unpredictable, showing up for work with alcohol on her breath and even carrying her gun to work, despite signs on the building outside that prohibited it. Many patients started to complain that they never got return phone calls if they left a message. She found out later that Daisy had told people not to worry about paying their bills as well, that they would be written off if the insurance company didn't cover them. Dealing with that situation had caused Laura some anxiety. She didn't like to confront people, but she had no choice but to fire Daisy. And there were the two patients she had met in her first week who made her wonder how safe the town really was.

On the morning of her second day at her new office, her first patient,

Mr. Elmwood, came in for a checkup. He was in his seventies, and he was partially deaf.

"Good morning, Mr. Elmwood. How are you today?" she asked.

"I'm still buying green bananas," he replied.

Laura laughed as she thought about what that implied, that he'd at least be around long enough for them to ripen so he could eat them. "Well, that's an optimistic purchase," she replied.

"I have to think that way at my age. I'm just glad to be alive, especially after what happened to me a while back. I thank God every day."

"What do you mean?" Laura asked.

"Well, I don't want to alarm you with my bad luck. I'm sure you're too busy for my story," he replied.

"Oh, no, go ahead. I have the time," she said, not knowing if her next patient had arrived.

"Well, I was sleeping a few months back, went to bed like normal, and woke up around 3:00 a.m. with a gun to my head. Because of my loss of hearing in my right ear, I didn't even hear anyone come in the house. I found out later they had originally just come to take the rims off my granddaughter's car, but they brought one of their friends along who talked them into coming inside and robbing me. Like I said, I'm just lucky to be alive."

"Wow, that's terrible. I'm glad you weren't hurt!" Laura replied.

"Yeah, they just tied me up and stole my TV and some cash out of my dresser drawer. I guess they realized I didn't really have much else to steal."

None of Laura's patients in California had ever told her anything like that. She was surprised to hear this kind of thing was happening in the small town of Jupiter.

Her next patient was a thirteen-year-old boy, brought in by his mom. His name was Billie. His mom said that Billie had been at the car wash with his eighteen-year-old brother, and they had been held up at gunpoint. She was concerned that he might be having anxiety because he couldn't sleep at all since the episode occurred. His brother seemed to be doing okay, but Billie was having nightmares.

"Billie, what happened?" Laura asked, hoping to get a better idea of the situation.

"Umm ... I was with my brother a couple of nights ago, and around seven o'clock, this guy came up to us and asked us for money. He noticed my brother's nice car, I guess. At first my brother just blew him off, but then the guy came back holding a gun. My brother said, 'Hold on, man. You don't want to do that. I'll give you some money, but you don't have to pull a gun on us. I've got my brother with me. Just be cool man.' So I guess the guy kind of relaxed and put the gun down. I think he saw my brother's US Marines bumper sticker at some point because he asked if he was in the marines, and my brother said yes. So then my brother gave him twenty dollars, and the guy walked away. We got out of there right away and called the police, but I don't think they found him."

"Okay, Mom, I can see why Billie is having difficulty sleeping. But the good news is that no one was hurt. I think it is absolutely normal to be having some anxiety, considering what happened. It sounds like you were both very brave," Laura said, now turning her attention to Billie, "I think after the initial shock of it wears off, you will feel much better. Most people that experience traumatic events do fine over time. There are those who do better with counseling, and that might be in order." Laura directed her attention back to Billie's mom. "I'd like to see how Billie does over the next two weeks. I recommend using a night light while he sleeps, if he doesn't have one already. I'd like to see if we can avoid using medications to help him sleep since he's so young. But time will tell. Go ahead and schedule a follow-up in two weeks so we can reassess Billie, but please call if anything changes or if you have any questions."

"Thank you, Doctor. I feel better already. I think Billie is a strong boy. I know he will do fine," Mom said encouragingly, mostly for Billie's sake.

"You're welcome. And Billie, I'm very proud of your bravery."

"Thank you, ma'am."

Her last encounter left Laura scratching her head. She just couldn't get over the fact that her last two patients had been victims of violent crimes. She started to wonder what she had gotten into. *What is up with this town?* she thought.

Later in that first week she had found a paper left behind on Dr. Freeman's desk that was a copy of a police report. It seemed that Dr. Freeman's office had been robbed while he and one of his employees were just getting to work one day. Since he opened at six in the morning, his office was the only one open. This incident had never been mentioned to

Laura, so finding that report, along with the other patient accounts of violence, had caused Laura great concern.

Ryan wasn't especially happy with living in Jupiter either. He was used to working hard all day and staying active, but now he was just bored. There really wasn't a lot to do in Jupiter and any time they wanted to go out, they would have to drive almost an hour to get to "civilization", as they called it. One of the only things they did together for physical activity was walk their dogs down the road to the lake and back, which was about two miles away. Unfortunately, Laura didn't feel safe even walking, due to one occasion when a car filled with young teenagers drove by. As it went further down the road, all of a sudden, Laura and Ryan heard gunshots coming from that direction. Ryan had said they were probably shooting at armadillos, or at least he hoped that was all it was.

Laura was offered an income that was only guaranteed for her first year of the job, and now, that would significantly decrease due to her practice not growing like it was supposed to. The company had guaranteed her all of Dr. Freeman's three thousand patients, but she'd only received two hundred of them. It wasn't until now, when the income was going to decrease, that she realized they might have a problem. They still had their home in California and were renting it out to a pastor and his wife. They had given them a break on the rent, but it was costing them several hundred dollars a month to do so. But they had felt that God had prompted them to rent their house to the pastor, and that was all he could afford.

For dinner that night, Ryan cooked his specialty—spaghetti and meatballs with homemade marinara sauce. It was Laura's favorite dish. When they sat down to eat, Laura couldn't help but bring up all of the difficulties they had experienced since the whole Stan fiasco. As she went through the list, she remembered the first tenant to whom they had rented their home. The heater had unfortunately stopped working in the middle of winter, and the man did not want to use the wood-burning stove. They tried to get it fixed as quickly as they could, but the man had a history of bipolar disorder and had gone down to the property manager's office and threatened his life. The police had to be called, but no one was hurt. The property manager decided he didn't want to manage their property anymore after that incident. Laura and Ryan shook their heads, as they were reminded of their "series of unfortunate events", as they called them.

"Do you ever wonder how we got where we are now?" Ryan asked Laura.

"Yes, but I know it was our own stupidity," she responded. "Hopefully, things will get better, and we will be wiser in the future,"

"I love you, Laura, and you know I'd do anything for you, even live here in Jupiter," Ryan added playfully.

In the heavenly realm, Dunamis summoned Laura's and Ryan's guardian angels. He knew that Laura and Ryan were not specifically aware yet of the spiritual warfare in which they were deeply involved. The agenda for the day was to discuss how to thwart off the pending attacks of Tat, the demon of impatience, and Furies, the demon of hate. They discussed the current situation and plans of the enemy that they were able to ascertain over the last eleven months through reconnaissance missions. The demons answered to Wink, the new chief commander over the south central portion of the United States. Wink had asked for the transfer when he saw that Ashkran had no intention of ever leaving his position as the chief commander in the Northwest. Wink's participation in the damnation of souls in the Olympia, Washington, battle had been so exemplary that he was given the opportunity to prove himself worthy of being a chief in his own right. Wink had been keeping score, and the demons were in the lead by a long shot. He felt quite comfortable tormenting Laura and Ryan as well and knew exactly what their weaknesses were. The demons had an advantage in that Laura and Ryan were no longer in a location controlled by the angelic realm. Through spiritual eyes, there was a twenty-five-foot-tall fiery ring around the Jupiter, Texas, area and a ten-mile perimeter that was patrolled by the demons of the 65th Battalion.

For the last three years, they had maintained control of the city and were in the process of expanding their borders. Recently, during their furtive missions, the angels had traveled to the demon world, where they overheard Wink talking with Tat about his priorities. His goal was always to cause as much destruction as possible by looking specifically for individuals who had a special mark only seen in the spiritual world. He knew that targeting those specific individuals would cause the greatest damage. The children of God could have many different kinds of marks. In the spiritual world, the children of God had a completely different appearance than in the physical world. They all appeared to be soft yellow moonlight in coloring and contained large, glowing red hearts deep within. They were all over fifteen feet tall and had glowing green eyes. *And, oh, if they only knew the power they had,* Wink had said over and over again as he conjured up and tapped together his grotesque tendrils. Their distinguishing feature, which could be seen in varying degrees or was absent altogether, was on their backs—a dark marking that looked like a spiral and ranged in color from bright indigo to deep black. The demons were aware that these markings meant that they had a special duty or purpose to fulfill; the exact details were unknown to them. But of all of the victims of Stan Powers's previously hatched conspiracy, only Laura and Ryan both had the deep indigo spirals on their backs, and so far, Tat and Furies had been doing a great job causing them to suffer.

"Well, Dunamis, since Laura and Ryan decided to move to Jupiter, we have had a difficult time protecting and defending them, since it is controlled by the 65th Battalion. We've lost a lot of skirmishes recently," said Willon, Laura's guardian angel.

"Also, they haven't necessarily been in God's will. Laura and Ryan also need help with learning how to wait for God's timing. If they had only remained where they were …" Trylon, Ryan's guardian angel said, his voice trailing off as he realized there was no use in having regrets over the past.

"My concern is keeping them safe until they are able to fulfill their purpose. We will continue to battle Tat and Furies by taking the offense, and by that I mean we will lay some groundwork for Laura and Ryan to see their strength. This will take some time. First, we need to expose them to God's Word. At this point they have no idea what kind of power they have, and we need to make them aware. We need to get them to the place where they are walking in God's power and not trying to do things in their own strength. We can begin by putting an idea into Ryan's and Laura's heads about finding a local church so they can get some direction," said Dunamis. "I know for a fact that there is a plan about to be launched by Furies. We will have to stay focused on breaking through the demonic barricade stretching over their location." He paused and then pleaded, "Just keep praying, Ryan and Laura. Keep praying."

CHAPTER 14

ON THE FOLLOWING SATURDAY, RYAN woke up with the memories of his dream the night before. In the dream, he was sitting in the front row at a church he had never seen before. He remembered the pastor pointing in his direction and saying *"Come to me, all who are weary, and I will give you rest."* Then he was motioned up to the platform where the pastor had him lie down on a couch. Next thing he knew, the sermon was over, and the pastor and his wife were waking him up, telling him he had missed the best part of the sermon and invited him back for the following week. They had said how important the message was that he missed, and he really needed to hear it.

When he told Laura about the dream, she said, "I've been thinking we should find a church soon, I think maybe your dream is confirmation."

"Okay, let's try to find one. We can do a search online to see if there's one close by."

The next day, Laura and Ryan were too tired to get up and visit a church. Ryan hadn't been feeling very well and didn't sleep much the night before. Laura had been up also, worried about him. *Besides,* she thought, *we still don't know where to go.*

Laura was glad it was Sunday and that she could stay home and relax. Ryan was sleeping in late, and she decided to make some chocolate chip cookies. She then decided to watch TV and came across a pastor preaching a sermon on the pit test. This caught her attention. His name was Pastor Morris, and he was talking about how God puts us through different tests in our lives to help us grow so we can accomplish our purpose. The pit test referred to when Joseph was thrown into a pit by his brothers, and it represented a trial in his life.

"I sure feel like I've been through several pit tests," Laura muttered to the empty room.

And almost as if in response to her comment, Pastor Morris then said, "And the good ... and the bad news is, we will keep taking the test over and over again until we pass it."

A surprised Laura looked up from her bowl of cookie dough and laughed out loud. She listened to the rest of the sermon and realized that Pastor Morris's church was in the Dallas area. She knew deep down that *that* was the church for them. Laura's cell phone rang at that moment, and she saw the name Paul come up on the screen. She hadn't heard from him since moving to Texas.

"Hello?" she said guardedly.

"Hi, Laura, it's been a while, I know. How are you guys doing?" Paul asked.

"Fine," she said, not knowing what else to say.

"Hey, the reason I'm calling is to let you guys know about an opportunity with which I have been presented to help the people who were victims of Stan's Ponzi scheme."

"What is it?" she asked.

"I'll send you an e-mail with more information, but the short of it is that there is a wealthy businessman looking for credit partners, and he heard about what happened to all of us with Stan. He wants to help us all get paid back and make us whole again. His name is Howard Holland, and he has a company called Eagle Funding Group. He's planning to use all of us as credit partners to start new businesses around the United States and the Bahamas. He wants to start with building multifamily dwellings in urban areas. If you are interested, I'll send you the paperwork to sign up," Paul explained.

"Yeah, you can send it. I'll take a look at it."

"The cool thing about it is that he will hire us as employees, and we will get a salary for five years and a company car."

"Sounds really good," Laura responded. "I'll be looking for your e-mail."

"See ya soon, Laura."

Later that day, Laura got the e-mail from Paul and looked it over. It looked like they had to sign over power of attorney for them to be able to borrow money for the projects. She decided it was worth at least listening to Mr. Holland's plan. She went to check on Ryan, and he was just waking up.

"How are you feeling, Ryan?"

"Not good. I have these sharp cramps in my lower abdomen. I have to keep my knees bent up so I can sleep, but I just can't get comfortable. I think I'd do better on the couch at night. I'm okay right now, but as soon as I eat something, the cramps come back. I think spicy food is making it worse," he said.

"Well, maybe you can have some soup or something. Hey, I just got a call from Paul," she added hesitatingly.

"Really? What did he want?" Ryan asked. "Is there new news about Stan?"

"No, he actually wanted to offer us an opportunity to get paid back from what Stan stole from us," she said.

"How so?" asked Ryan.

Laura explained the conversation and the e-mail, and they decided to let Paul know they were interested in hearing more about it. Laura e-mailed Paul the next day.

Later that day, Paul e-mailed back to say they were having a conference call the next day at noon. "Will that work for you guys?" he typed.

"Yes," she responded.

Later that day she got a response. "I'll send the conference call number and code later today so you can have it to log into the call," Paul typed. "Have a good day!"

The next day at 11:45 a.m., Laura went home from work for lunch and to get on the conference call with Ryan. They put the phone on speaker at 11:59 a.m. and called into the conference call.

When they were prompted, they said their names, which were recorded and used in the announcement of their joining the call. *Ding. Laura and Ryan have just entered the conference call. Please join the other nine people on the call,* a robotic female voice said.

"Hey, Laura, this is Paul. We have Howard Holland and his daughters on the phone, as well as a colleague, Mike Starr, and the president and secretary of Eagle Funding Group, Chuck Shoeman and Carla Simpson, respectively. Also, I have my friends Joey and Natalie Grimm. They also lost money like Ryan and Laura. I was fortunate enough to meet Howard through a real estate business associate of mine. I'm excited for you all to hear what he has to say."

"Hello, everyone," Ryan and Laura said in unison.

"Hey," several people responded at once. After a few seconds of silence, a throat cleared and a quiet male voice spoke.

"Thank you, everyone, for joining us today," said Howard Holland. Laura noticed right away he had a deep voice and seemed to be an older gentleman. It was difficult to hear, however, and she had to strain to hear him speak. She figured it was due to being on a conference call with so many other people.

Howard continued. "I would like to introduce my daughters, Chris and Angela Scott. They are both very young, but I am doing this to help them learn how to build a company and to leave them a legacy. They will be put in charge of handling a lot of the details and running the company eventually. I'm doing all of this for my children. I don't want anything for myself. I appreciate everyone being patient with them in the meantime." Laura wasn't sure why his daughters had a different last name, but she didn't think this was the appropriate time to ask.

One of the young girl said, "Hi, everyone". The prideful tone in her voice was unmistakable. It sounded like she was in her late teens or early twenties, Laura ascertained by the sound of the voice.

"I have an older daughter, Whitney, as well. She is not able to be on the call today." Howard's speech was measured, Laura observed, as he continued. "My friend Paul here told me about what happened to him and to some of you on the phone call today. It's a terrible thing. What I have to discuss with you today is a new concept. My company is going to be purchasing and merging with other companies in order to start building multifamily homes for veterans in large urban areas, starting with Detroit. As some of you may or may not know, Detroit is suffering. I grew up in Detroit and once even gave the city two million dollars. I sometimes wonder if that was too generous, but nonetheless, I did it in order to help the city. Currently, I don't travel to Detroit, since I know so many people there. I try to keep a low profile. I pay a publicist six thousand dollars a month to keep my name out of the papers. But I'd like to help some of you by giving you an opportunity. You would all be credit partners, and we will borrow the money to assist in buying our first company, Gate Steele. We are ready to close on the transaction and just need twenty thousand dollars for escrow. By owning our own construction companies, we will be able to save money and grow quicker. By everyone allowing us to borrow on their personal credit, we can close the transaction and do a refinance to take away their personal liability. I'd like to restructure the financing using an investor who will help us with the bigger transactions. He has connections with big-time investors, who will be putting up hundreds of millions of dollars. Once we have our first company, we can turn around and get the investor to put up a large sum of money, in tranches, to help us purchase other companies. Then, using securities, we will have our company go public. I also have a lender with whom I have worked for over thirty years to help us finance the companies. There is a lot more to it. I'm just giving you the bare bones of the transaction." Howard paused and then asked, "Any questions so far?"

"Yes, this is Laura. I have a question, Mr. Holland,"

"You can call me Howard, Doctor. What is your question?"

"Likewise, you can call me Laura. Howard, I hope this doesn't sound like a rude question, but why do you want to help us?"

"Consider me a philanthropist. I'm in a position where I could be the one to help you, Laura, or the one to put the last nail in your coffin. I prefer to help you. I know what it's like to be where you are. And I'm as serious as a heart attack when I say that." When Howard finished answering, no one spoke. He resumed.

"Not only will I pay everyone a salary and give them a company car, but I would like to give back, to the first ten people who sign up, the total amount they lost in the Ponzi scheme of Mr. Stan Powers. Just send us some proof of the amount you lost, and we will make sure you get that back once the first transaction closes. Obviously, we will be supplying promissory notes for any and all money that you borrow for the projects," Howard said.

"Hi, Howard, this is Natalie. How much money would we have to borrow?"

"Well, not everyone will have to borrow money. We will have to look at everyone's credit score and determine that number. I also want to help people raise their credit scores so we will be able to continue to borrow as needed. Eventually, though, we will get rid of the personal guarantees. Once we go public, we will not need to use your personal credit anymore," Howard concluded.

Laura put the phone on mute and looked at Ryan. "What do you think?"

"I don't know. I guess we could fill out the paperwork and see what they want to do."

Laura took the phone off mute just as Paul was asking if anyone was interested in moving forward.

"Natalie, here. We will have to think about it."

"Yes, Ryan and I will submit the paperwork after looking over a few things," said Laura.

"Thank you for your time. I will have my daughter Chris e-mail you the notes from today's call and give you all of our contact information. She will be your direct contact. Have a good day, every one."

The automated voice came on the line and reported, *Howard Holland has left the conference call.* Then, the voice began to say the names of the other callers in sequence as they hung up, one after the next.

CHAPTER 15

THE NEXT DAY WAS SATURDAY. When Laura got up she checked her e-mail and found one from Chris Scott. She sent the contact information for everyone who was on the call, as well as contact information for her older sister Whitney Bates. Laura and Ryan didn't know very much about Mr. Holland. Was he married? Where did he live? What were his credentials?

Laura was sitting at her desk in their large master bedroom and decided to talk to Ryan about her concerns. She couldn't find him in the house and went out back to the shop, where she could hear hammering from forty yards away. As she walked in the door, his back was to her. She came up from behind him and put her arms around his waist. He didn't act surprised in the least as he turned to give her a kiss.

"Good morning, honey. Did you sleep well?" Ryan asked.

"Yes. How about you?"

"Not so good. I couldn't fall asleep. I had to sleep on the couch for part of the night. I think I only slept for two hours. I don't know what's wrong with me," Ryan said with a look of concern on his face.

"I don't know either. You know we haven't been eating very well lately. Let's try to eat better and see if that makes a difference. I'll buy some more vegetables and stop buying all of the junk food."

"That sounds good. I think it's time to start taking better care of ourselves," Ryan agreed.

"You know, Ryan, I've been thinking. I'd like to get more information about Howard. He's going to learn a lot about us after we fill out all of this paperwork. It seems reasonable for us to want to know more about him. Maybe I can e-mail and ask him about his background. It won't hurt to ask, will it?"

"I think it's reasonable. Go for it," Ryan replied. Laura went back into the house, got on her computer, and composed an e-mail to Howard Holland.

Dear Howard,

I hope this e-mail finds you well. Thank you for your time yesterday on the conference call. I was hoping to learn more about you. As you know, we have been put through a rough time and have had our trust violated by someone we thought was a friend. It would put our minds at ease to learn more about you and your family. Also, we would like to know more about your background and previous business transactions so we can know more about your experience in business. Also, would you consider meeting with us in person? Where are you located currently? Ryan and I would be interested in meeting with you in the near future. I greatly appreciate you answering my questions.

Sincerely,
Laura

Laura clicked on the Send button and also sent a copy of the e-mail to Howard's daughters. After sending the e-mail, Laura filled out the paperwork and sent it to Chris. She knew Ryan and she had excellent credit scores. They always paid their bills on time, and they certainly didn't like to borrow money if they didn't have to. She hoped they wouldn't have to borrow too much money. But at least she was consoled by the fact that Howard only wanted them to borrow it short term.

The next day, Laura got an e-mail from Paul: " I got an e-mail from Howard. He would like to have a brief call with you and your husband, if possible. His daughter Chris and I would be on the call as well. How would tonight at 7:00 work for you?"

She responded with a brief e-mail of her own:"That would be great."

At 7:05 Laura's phone rang. She and Ryan were waiting for the call as they lay on the bed with the phone on speaker.

"Hello?" Said Laura.

"Hi, Laura, this is Chris. I have my dad, Howard Holland, on the line, as well as Paul."

After greetings all around, Howard spoke softly.

"Hello. I wanted to respond to Laura's e-mail. At first I was taken aback by all of the questions, but I decided to not fly off of the handle because I understand that you guys have been put through a lot. First of all, we are dealing with securities here; this is serious stuff. I would never do anything to put my daughters or myself in danger of anything that would seem inappropriate or threaten our livelihood. Never."

Laura and Ryan looked at each other in silence with eyebrows slightly raised. Laura noticed Howard's tone was very serious.

"I do not currently travel, due to my health—or lack of it, I should say. I have diabetes and some complications from it. I have to stay in the area due to having dialysis once a week. I am living in Miami, Florida, at the moment. I consider myself a recluse—I don't even let my daughters visit. As far as my experience goes, I am retired. I spent years doing deals across the United States and in areas such as the Bahamas and Saint Lucia and so forth. I am an African American, so I have faced a lot of prejudice in my lifetime. I've been partners and formed companies with Jewish partners. There was a certain strategy behind that. I knew having a Jewish name usually helped one do well in business; it's a stereotype for a reason. I was the chief financial officer of one such company called Goldberg, Smith, and Stein. We built properties such as apartments and hotels. I will never forget one occasion where we were about to purchase a hotel in New York City. The buyers wanted to meet with us in person. When they realized I was a black man, they changed their minds about selling it to us. I cried that day … bawled like a baby. I was crushed. But you know what they say about adversity: 'There is no education like adversity.' But I used that adversity to spur me to do better. I believe that I am a success today because of that incident. My mother was the one who helped me the most. She believed in me and encouraged me when I was at my lowest. She is the reason I formed our family trust, the Mildred Howard Family Trust. It is the instrument that we will be using to purchase some of the properties as well. We have a lot of assets in the trust that we may need to use as collateral."

There was silence for a few seconds before anyone responded. It was Chris who broke the silence.

"Dad, did you want to talk to Ryan about his application?"

"Oh, yes," Howard said, changing gears. "I am looking over the application, and I see you have a background in tree work. Do you have a contractor's license?"

"Yes," Ryan said, though he was still thinking about what Howard had told them about his past. He was interested in looking into some of the previous deals Howard had made.

"I would like to use your credit in the capacity to purchase some of the construction companies. We will have you borrow forty thousand dollars. We will be able to close on Gate Steele and also some other construction companies we have been looking at. I haven't heard yet from the other couple, the Grimms, but they will also be helping to purchase those properties. At this point, Laura, we won't need you to borrow any money, but you will still get a salary. I'll have Mike Starr contact you, Ryan. He will be the one borrowing money on your behalf."

"Um, Howard, I was wondering how long it's going to take to purchase this Gate Steele property?" Laura asked cautiously.

"That will depend on how quickly we can get the funding, Laura. Are there any other questions?" Howard asked.

"None I can think of," Ryan said.

"Good. It looks like we have been on the phone for over an hour. I have a lot of work to do. Have a nice night, everyone." Howard hung up the phone.

"I'm going to look into the Mildred Holland Family Trust, and see if I can find anything about it online. I'm also going to look into some of the companies he mentioned in his past. I know Howard would never do anything to put his daughters in danger of getting in trouble. I think it's wise, though, to see what we can find out before moving forward," said Laura.

"I agree," said Ryan.

The next day Laura did an extensive search online. She was able to find a Mildred Holland living in Detroit but nothing else. She tried to do a search on Howard Holland and came up with one who lived in Miami and was related to a Mildred Holland. Later that day, Mike called Ryan with the name of a loan officer at a local bank in Dallas.

"Hi, Ryan, how are you?" Mike asked in his warm Southern drawl.

"Fine, and you?" .

"I'm doing great. I just went for an hour run, and I'm about to have my second cup of coffee. I wanted to let you know that you should expect a call from someone at Texas National Bank in Dallas. He is ready to lend you twenty thousand dollars and just wants to ask you a few questions about your application."

Ryan was a little surprised that someone was willing to lend him money so easily. He felt a little bit uneasy about it, but knew it was only short term.

"Okay, Mike. Thanks for letting me know. By the way, how did you get involved with Howard?"

"Oh, I was approached by Chris, actually, who had been working with Eagle Funding Group only for a short time. I was working on another project, and Howard asked me personally to oversee his daughter's work and teach her about the financing world."

"Good to hear. It's going to be interesting to watch this deal close," Ryan said.

"Oh yes, it's just the beginning. I'll be in touch shortly about a couple of credit cards for which we will be applying for you as well."

"I'll be here," Ryan said.

In a couple of weeks, they had borrowed the full forty thousand dollars on Ryan's behalf for the closing of Gate Steele. They had several additional conference calls in the meantime, and it looked like, for the moment, Ryan and Laura were the only ones to sign up as credit partners. Chris had called, with Howard on the line, to let Laura know that they were going to have her borrow a small amount of money as well. Howard had some new ideas for them about the projects. Eventually, they had a conference call to discuss them.

"Hi again, everyone," Howard said to the group from Eagle Funding, as well as Ryan, Laura, Mike, and Paul, with his daughters on the phone as well. "I have decided to create a medical component to complement the multifamily dwellings. Since we are fortunate to have Laura here with us, she will be able to provide the leadership to open the clinics in the dwellings."

Laura was slightly surprised at this new idea, but it seemed to make perfect sense to her, and it grew on her immediately.

"I will be asking Laura to find colleagues that she can bring on board to help us structure the clinics, which I would like to be complete medical facilities, with the full range of services. In order to do this, we will have Laura borrow money as well, which, again, will be very short term. I have brought one of my business partners to the call today to meet everyone. He will be assisting with the transactions. His name is Adam Jameson. We have worked together for many years. I'd like him to introduce himself."

"Hello, everyone. I look forward to working with you. I have been in the lending business for over thirty years and was excited to get a call from Howard, inviting me to join in this venture," said Adam. From the sound of his voice, Laura wasn't sure Adam was the kind of man who could get excited. He continued. "Laura, I will be in contact with you shortly. But I will be sending you an application for Country Bank, as well as something called a bank statement loan. I will also want to see if we can maximize your borrowing on your current credit cards. This money will be used to help purchase some medical companies that I have had Mike research." Adam began to cough and had to put his phone on mute. Howard continued for Adam,

"We will be in touch, Laura."

"What are we doing about paying Ryan's first payments on his loan and credit cards?" asked Laura. They had been instructed to send the money from the loan and also the credit cards to Chris. That was the thing that made them the most uneasy, but it was necessary.

"I will have Chris make all payments so you won't have to worry about it. I will make sure she pays them on time. For all of the credit partners, Eagle Funding will have a department that is responsible for making timely payments. But for now, since we only have the two of you, we will make Chris responsible for it," said Howard.

"What about the closing of Gate Steele?" asked Laura with curiosity.

"That is another issue altogether," said Howard. "Chris, what is the status of that closing?"

"I don't know, Dad."

"Mr. Starr, what is the status of that closing?"

"Well, Mr. Holland, on the last call I got from the broker, I was told they were waiting for you to give them the five million cash."

"That's what Adam is going to be helping us with. We will be talking to his private investor to borrow the money for that. In exchange, he will get a certain percentage of shares when we go public," replied Howard.

"No problem, Howard. Let's go over the transaction after this call," said Adam.

"I will let you know the closing date, Laura, once we solidify the investor's contract. Have a good night, everyone," said Howard.

"Bye, Howard," said Laura.

"Adam sounds like he really knows what he is doing," Laura said to Ryan.

"Yes, I think so too. It's going to be interesting. I hope you won't have to borrow a lot of money. I don't like borrowing so much."

"Me either."

CHAPTER *16*

The weapons we fight with are not the weapons
of the world. On the contrary, they have
divine power to demolish strongholds.
—2 Corinthians 10:4

One Month Later

LAURA WAS SITTING AT HER desk, waiting for her next patient to arrive. The patient was already ten minutes late, which, unfortunately, usually meant that the patient was not going to show up. She was feeling a little stressed over the low number of patients she had on the schedule. She knew she had to do something to bring in more patients. Deep down, she was hoping these new projects would come together quickly so she could start getting her salary. They were told their salaries would start within the next month. In the meantime, it was time to start making payments for Ryan's credit cards and loan. Laura was uncomfortable with not being able to make them. She didn't know if Chris would be responsible, due to her young age. She decided she would talk to Howard about making the payments herself for now, just to make sure everything was paid on time. She didn't want to take the chance of hurting her credit score. She had also been contacted by Adam and had signed the application for the bank statement loan for forty thousand dollars. The company was starting to take out five hundred dollars a day directly from her business bank account to repay it. Laura was hoping the Gate Steele deal would close so they could get back their money and get rid of their debt once and for all. Mike had found a group of five medical companies that Howard wanted her to visit with Mike before purchasing them. She was supposed to leave the following week. She knew she was going to have to borrow another larger amount to purchase the companies and was waiting for one of her applications to be processed from Country Bank. It was making Laura a little stressed.

When Laura got home from work, she found Ryan lying on the floor in their bedroom, writhing in pain, holding his lower abdomen and moaning.

"Ryan, what's wrong?" she yelled as she ran into the room, purse dropping to the floor.

"My stomach … it hurts so bad … I can't eat anything. I think I've lost about ten pounds since this all started," he moaned.

"Why didn't you tell me? I thought you were feeling better," Laura said with concern.

"I keep thinking I'm getting better, but then I try to eat something and the pains return. I was just trying to eat an egg salad sandwich."

"We should go to the ED, Ryan."

"No, I'll feel better soon. Let me see how I feel in a couple of hours," he replied with tears in his eyes.

"I've never seen you like this, Ryan; it's not normal." Laura thought for a moment and then said, "I'll give you until tonight. In the meantime, let me get you some Pepto-Bismol. Did you take anything else?"

"Just Tylenol. I can't eat anything. I can only drink water, and even that makes my stomach hurt."

"Well, I think you should just lie down and rest for now."

"Yeah, I can't do anything else. I'll just lie down on the couch in the living room," he said in agreement.

A few hours later, when Laura was ready for bed, she went into the living room to see how Ryan was feeling. She tiptoed over to the couch and saw that he was asleep. Their little black schipperke, Boo, was curled up next to him. She didn't want to wake them up, so she slowly tiptoed out of the room. She was thankful that he seemed to be feeling better. As she lay down to go to sleep, she prayed for Ryan to get better and for their new projects to close soon. As she looked at the foot of the bed and saw two of her cats, she added humorously, *and please don't let the cats attack my feet in the middle of the night. Amen.*

Around 3:00 a.m., Laura woke up to Ryan's voice. He had walked into their room and fell to the floor. He began to groan.

"I can't take this anymore. I feel like I'm going to die," Ryan yelled in agony.

Laura jumped out of bed and turned the light on. " I'm putting on my shoes, and we are going to the ED. Just hang on, Ryan."

"I'm trying," he moaned.

"Are you able to get up, babe?" she asked.

"Yeah." Ryan slowly got off the floor and walked with his upper body bent forward. He had to stop a couple of times as he walked out the back door and got into the car. He was only in his running shorts and an old T-shirt, but he didn't care.

At that very moment, Wink was putting thoughts of fear of death and desertion into Laura's mind and at the same time attacking Ryan's physical body. He didn't need help from any other demons for this attack. *Furies is busy working his plan anyway,* Wink thought. He was able to capture their guardian angels, Willon and Trylon, by a blitzkrieg and easily wrapped them in his black webbing. He temporarily had them bound and suspended over a large, volcanic, fiery pit. There were explosions of lava going on around them. He knew they would break free eventually, but he had a special satisfaction in being able to overtake them so easily. They would be wounded deeply by the burns, which he hoped would permanently maim them.

Laura drove up to the ED and parked in the front. There were only a couple of cars parked out front. When they walked in, the nurse working in triage recognized her.

"Hello, Dr. Carroll. How can I help you?" the nurse named Bonnie asked.

"I brought my husband, Ryan, in to be evaluated. He is having some abdominal pains," Laura said.

Bonnie's countenance fell as she realized this was a personal visit for Laura, not a professional one. "Oh my goodness, let me get you checked in right away." She came around the desk through the door. "Please have a seat, Mr. Carroll." Bonnie directed him to a seat in the triage area.

As Laura was checking Ryan in, Dr. Perry came around the corner and saw Laura sitting at the triage window."

"What brings you in, Dr. Carroll?" he asked.

"My husband. He's having abdominal pain."

"I'll take him back right now. Come with me, please."

Laura helped Ryan walk back to the exam room. They walked past several empty beds and one closed curtain, which Laura assumed was a sign of a patient behind it.

"Tell me about your symptoms," Dr. Perry said.

Ryan lay down on the hospital bed and told Dr. Perry about his symptoms. Dr. Perry asked several routine questions in the process: On a scale of one to ten, ten being the most excruciating pain you can imagine, what score would you give the pain? When did the pain begin? What makes it better? What makes it worse?

After Dr. Perry did a complete physical exam, he ordered IV fluids and a shot of Toradol for the pain. "I think we should get an abdominal CT scan, Laura," said Dr. Perry

"That sounds good," Laura agreed. She knew it would help to put Ryan's mind at ease. She had a feeling deep down that a lot of his symptoms were due to stress, but she had a voice in her head telling her that she might be missing something.

After an hour, Ryan was taken down to the radiology department for his CT scan. After the scan, Laura and Ryan waited for the results back in the examination room, while praying for his healing. Ryan slowly began to feel better after the Toradol shot, and he fell asleep. Laura sat in the chair next to his bed, holding his hand. She was having difficulty keeping her eyes open. It was in the vague haziness between suspension of consciousness and awakening that Laura heard voices.

Ryan's not going to make it. He's going to keep losing weight until he wastes away. You'll be alone for the rest of your life. In her mind's eye, she was walking slowly through a dark hallway where the air was filled with a musty scent. She was walking on uneven pavement toward a lighted room. When she arrived at the doorway, she looked in and saw Ryan, with his body cavity torn open and his intestines spilling out on the floor. Laura heard herself screaming, *No, no, no!*

It was almost six in the morning when Dr. Perry walked into the room, looked down at his chart, and said in a loud voice, "Good news. The CT scan is perfectly normal."

Laura's head shot up like she had been slapped, and she sat up in her chair. It took a few seconds for her mind to process Dr. Perry's words. She wasn't sure if she had been screaming out loud or not, but she didn't care, and Dr. Perry didn't say anything about it. She was relieved to hear Dr. Perry's report. Ryan began to slowly stir, and Dr. Perry walked out of the room.

"Did you hear that, Ryan? The CT is completely normal," Laura said with a smile growing on her face. Ryan yawned and raised his arms over his head.

"That's good news. Thank you, Jesus! I'm feeling much better. I'd love to go home now." He yawned the words more than spoke them. "I'm sorry you had to lose out on sleep on my account," he said in his normal voice.

"I'm just glad you're okay, Ryan. I think we will have to watch our diets more closely … and watch our stress levels," Laura suggested.

"Come on. Let's go home. I'll drive," Ryan said.

"I think you had better get out of that hospital gown first!" Laura laughed as the image of the backside of Ryan walking down the hall in his flimsy gown came to her mind.

CHAPTER 17

It was Friday morning in early September, the morning that Laura and Ryan were supposed to go to Miami to meet with Mike and visit one of the five medical companies that Howard wanted to purchase. He had created a new entity named the Laura Carroll Medical Company, which he had incorporated in Florida. Laura was going to be the owner and president of the company. Howard had asked for the resumes of some of her colleagues to see who could be hired to run the companies, along with some of his own colleagues. The plan was to use the medical acquisitions as templates to assist in developing their medical clinics, as well as utilize the expertise of the individual owners for the short term. So far, several people had seemed interested in helping them with their project. Howard had his daughter Chris send a one hundred million dollar credit letter from Eagle Funding Group for the Laura Carroll Medical Company for Laura to sign.

The temperature was unseasonably cool. Laura had also checked the weather for Miami, which was also going to be partly sunny and in the high seventies. She was glad her clothes didn't stick to her skin as soon as she stepped out of the back door and didn't feel the beads of sweat dripping down the middle of her back. She was also pleased to not have to wear her hair in a ponytail for the first time since the summer heat started. The company they were visiting today was simply called Miami Imaging. After dropping off their dogs at the kennel, they made their way to the airport one hour before their flight was supposed to take off. Laura was a little nervous to meet Mike in person and to visit the company. They had never done anything like this before. But that was what made it exciting to them. By now, with all of the conference calls, Laura and Ryan felt comfortable with Mike. Chris had made the travel arrangements for them using one of Ryan's credit cards on one of the discount travel websites and had gotten them a great deal. They were supposed to meet at the airport and travel by a chartered town car to the hotel and then off to Miami Imaging, where the owners and their broker were waiting. Howard had said to leave a lot of the talking to Mike, which suited Laura just fine. She was hoping to learn from this initial meeting so she could gain more confidence as time went on and more companies were visited.

Ryan was still having abdominal pains on occasion. He had lost twenty pounds at his lowest and was now only starting to slowly regain his weight. He could go for a week or two without any symptoms, but out of the blue, he would have a flare-up that would leave him curled up in a ball on the bed for hours, grimacing with pain. Laura continued to think this was stress-related due to their current financial situation and all of the recent ordeals they had endured. She didn't think it was worth mentioning any of this to Howard or Mike. She and Ryan were still waiting for their salaries to kick in from Eagle Funding Group. She was hoping that this visit would be successful and spur the process. Howard had said their investor was going to be out of the country for a week when she last asked about the Gate Steele transaction. He alleviated her concerns when he told her the closing date was going to be in two or three weeks at the most.

The flight was uneventful, and Laura and Ryan arrived at their gate on time and proceeded to the baggage claim to see if they could find Mike. They had not seen a picture of him but had agreed to meet at the baggage claim. They only took carry-on bags with them, so they would not need to wait for their luggage to be unloaded. They walked to the conveyor belt for Mike's flight and started to look for anyone who appeared to be looking for someone. Finally, they saw a thin white male with a light tan suit, checkered orange shirt, and dark brown tie walking toward them. He had black rimmed glasses and was carrying his laptop in one hand and a small black roller suitcase in the other. At first Laura thought, *That can't be him. Mike is a black man.* She asked Ryan if he thought that was Mike. He nodded, and she laughed to herself as she realized that the person she had always pictured as a black man in her mind was as white as a white man could be. She was too embarrassed to tell Ryan about her faulty imaginings.

"Hi, folks. Are you Ryan and Laura?" Mike asked in his charming Southern drawl.

"Yes, we are. You must be Mike," Ryan answered. "Great to finally meet you, Mike."

After they shook hands, they found their driver waiting for them on the curb with a sign on which their names had been written in red marker.

"How was your trip, Mike?" Laura asked.

"Oh, it was better than expected, considering the airline." Mike chuckled. "I'm not too fond of Soaring Airlines. I've had a few delays with them. I'm just glad that today we were all on time. So, anyway, Laura, I wanted to go over a few things with you before the meeting so you know what we are looking for in these individual companies. Please ask as many questions as you can. Howard will want a complete write-up of your observations when we return."

"That's no problem, Mike. That's one thing I know I can do," she responded. They pulled up to the hotel, and the driver got out to open the door for them.

"Great. Let's meet in the lobby after you have the chance to check in and take your belongings to your room. I'll be down there on my laptop when you guys are ready to go." Mike asked the driver to wait for them so he could take them to Miami Imaging.

After checking in, Laura and Ryan headed up to their hotel room.

"I guess I'm just here for moral support," Ryan declared with a matter-of-fact tone. "I don't know the first thing about imaging facilities. You're the expert today."

"Yeah, I guess so, but I'm not sure what to expect from Mike. I guess we will just listen to what he tells them and follow his lead."

"Guess so," Ryan said.

By 1:30 p.m., they had arrived at the imaging facility. They were right on time, which was important from Laura's perspective. When they walked to the front door they were greeted by Marvin Leavy. He was the broker for the imaging center. There were three owners, but only two were able to make the meeting, John and Larry. The third owner was out of town visiting her sick mother, they said.

"Well, hello. You must be Mike," said Marvin, extending his hand.

"Hello, Marvin, it's nice to meet you," Mike said as he held his hand out to shake Marvin's. "Let me introduce Dr. Carroll and her husband,

Ryan. They, as well as I, are very much looking forward to seeing your facility today."

"Yes, we have been looking forward to this meeting. This is John Rogers and Larry Sullivan," Marvin said, introducing his clients.

"It's nice to meet you both. It looks like you have a great facility here," said Mike. Laura and Ryan smiled and nodded in agreement. "Why don't we take a tour, Marvin?" Mike said as they walked into the lobby area.

"Yes, sir," said Marvin.

During the tour, Laura asked John and Larry about their equipment, the MRI machine as well as the CT scanner. They had just purchased the MRI system, which had better resolution than most of the older models. John said that everything was upgraded less than a year earlier. They walked through the waiting room, and Laura asked them about the volume of patients. Larry said they had very good connections with a couple of local law firms and were able to get a lot of business from patients who had been in motor vehicle accidents or had suffered on-the-job injuries.

After the tour, Marvin led them into a room with a conference table and said, "Please have a seat, everyone. We can get into more details about the financials after we get the accountant to pull together some reports for the last three years." Changing the subject, Marvin said, "I must say, Mike, I was quite surprised to see Howard Holland's name on one of the e-mails you sent to me. How is he involved in this? I knew him years ago I remember when he came to a meeting once with his daughters during the purchase of a property in New York City. He is the hardest worker I know. So how is he doing?"

"Fairly well. He's semi-retired, but you know what that means ... he is working only twelve hours a day now instead of twenty-four. He has some health problems, though. I've told him he needs to rest more," said Mike. "But let's get back to the imaging center for a minute. We have recent funding through one of Howard's business associates to purchase many medical companies, including yours. We are looking forward to purchasing your facility, along with several others that we are planning to visit in the next few weeks. I would like to see the financials for the past few months. I want to look at the business income since the purchase of the new MRI system."

"Absolutely, Mike, I'll leave that to the accountant. Do you need anything else?"

"Yes, I will need a list of all of the equipment, please. As part of the financing, Howard wants to obtain a loan based on the equipment value."

"I'm sure we can get that to you," Larry responded.

"Well, then I think that will be it for now. Oh, one more thing … where would you guys like to go to dinner tonight?"

When they returned home from Miami, Laura put together a report about the imaging center and her impressions. She mentioned in her report that one of the owners, John Rogers, would definitely be a great asset moving forward to help with the transition of the companies. She and Ryan had a good trip, but she was glad to be home. Howard and Chris were very pleased with her report. All of the concerns Laura had about Howard were put to rest when she heard what the broker had to say about him, but she did not know—nor could she have known—that it was the demon Tat who conveniently put the thought in Marvin's head so he confused Howard with another acquaintance of his altogether.

Chris put out an e-mail inviting everyone for a conference call that evening to give an update on the status of the Gate Steele purchase, the purchase of the medical companies, and some other issues. Laura hoped that those other issues included a discussion of receiving their salaries. It was time to make another payment to the loan companies for both of their loans, and they were waiting for Laura's $250,000 loan to close in the meantime. On the conference call, Howard guaranteed that her payments would not be late. Laura assumed that Howard might have to use his own money to pay her debts if it came down to the wire.

"As part of an update, I would like Mike to review the Gate Steele purchase as well as review the visit to the Miami imaging center," said Howard.

"Sure," said Mike, and he proceeded to let them know how the visit went with Marvin. Then he updated them on the Gate Steele purchase. "It looks like we will have to put the Gate Steele purchase on hold, temporarily. The owners are having cold feet about the strategy we are employing to purchase them. They just aren't sophisticated enough to understand why we are structuring the financing the way we are. But they will come around. In the meantime, Howard wishes to move forward with Ryan's new company, the Ryan Carroll Construction Company. We have several construction companies we wish to purchase in Detroit and would like Ryan to visit those, along with Paul and Mike."

"My daughter Chris will also be traveling to Detroit in two weeks to see the companies," added Howard.

Laura wondered about their salaries. She was starting to get concerned about the new loan she was taking out for the purchase of the medical companies. They would need some of that money to pay Ryan's and her loan payments in a few days. In the meantime, it bothered her that the Gate Steele purchase hadn't transpired as Howard had guaranteed.

"I will have Chris set up the trip for everyone. Laura, we will have to use your credit card to cover the expenses. Please give Chris your password online for the card in case she needs to check your balance before making a purchase. I did want to let you know that my daughter Whitney is also applying for a loan for one hundred thousand dollars to help with the purchase of the Detroit projects. It shouldn't be long before we obtain the funds for that loan. In the meantime, though, I appreciate your cooperation. You and Ryan are the best credit partners one could ever hope to find. I'll have my daughter Chris call you if she has any questions," Howard stated.

"Okay, Howard," Laura agreed. "But when do you think we can count on closing my loan? I'm assuming we need that money not only to pay our credit cards but to also close on the medical companies."

"Yes, it should be this week. In the meantime, I want Mike to visit the other medical companies this week so we can expedite things. I know you want to close a deal. Believe me, no one wants that more than I do, and I'm working night and day to make it happen," Howard said. "Oh, Laura will you be available for a quick call with me later? I'll call you in thirty minutes. I just have a few more things to go over."

"Sure, Howard. I'll be waiting," Laura said.

After two hours, Laura realized Howard wasn't going to call, so she went to bed.

CHAPTER *18*

THE FOLLOWING WEEK COULDN'T COME too quickly for Laura. She had gotten updates from Mike about the companies he had visited as well as their current financials. He had spent a lot of time talking with John, one of the owners of Miami Imaging. John was really interested in participating and helping in any way he could to close the sale of his company. The other owners seemed to be giving him a hard time because it was taking longer than usual to close the transaction, and things seemed to move along slowly. Laura knew it would take time to purchase all of the companies at the same time, and she was looking forward to seeing how Howard planned on closing them. All of the companies looked good to her; she wasn't the expert on evaluating companies for their worth, like Mike and Howard were. As much as she was going to miss Ryan, she was anticipating a rewarding trip to Detroit. She hoped things would go well, as they had in Miami. Then, finally, they would be able to close on the companies so they could start building the multifamily dwellings. She had thought it quite interesting that each of their backgrounds seemed to fit so perfectly with what Howard wanted to do. Deep down, she wondered if this was what she was always meant to do.

While in Detroit, Ryan, Paul, Mike, and Chris were supposed to meet with the president of a real estate consulting company called Trixlar Partners, who was a personal friend of Howard's. His name was Randy Getz. He was going to only be in the city for one day, and they wanted to schedule their other company visits around his schedule. Howard had told them it was just a quick meet-and-greet. They also were supposed to meet with a real estate agent named Ben Campbell who was going to give them a tour of the city and the various projects that Howard had been working on with Trixlar Partners.

They were all supposed to meet at the airport. Ryan was interested in meeting Chris, Howard's daughter. He had met both Mike and Paul, but this would be the first visit with Chris. He knew she would be taking notes on everyone and everything and would let her father know her impressions, so Ryan wanted to make a good one. He also wanted to learn a little bit about Howard from Chris, since Howard seemed to be such an enigma. Mike had told Ryan previously that neither he nor Paul had ever met her or any of Howard's daughters, nor had they met Howard. He said, in fact, that he didn't think anyone had met Howard in person.

When Ryan arrived to Detroit, he walked down to the baggage claim and waited to meet with Mike and Paul. He was hoping they could find Chris together. While he was waiting, he saw a tall, very young, thin black female picking a fuchsia bag up off of the conveyor belt about twenty feet away. She had black hair to her shoulders and a pink barrette holding back her hair on each side. She was wearing pink heels with a white suit and a bright pink blouse with its ruffles peeking through at her neckline. When she picked up her bag, he noticed she also had bright pink fingernails. *I bet that's her,* he thought. *She must like pink.* As she was putting the luggage strap of her bag on her shoulder, Ryan saw Mike approaching, and he noticed her as well. He watched Mike ask if she was Chris and saw her affirmative response and nod of the head. At that moment, Mike noticed Ryan watching them and motioned to Chris to look in his direction. They walked toward Ryan together.

"Hi, you must be Ryan," Chris said as she put out her hand in an elegant manner for Ryan to shake.

"Yes, and you must be Chris. I have to say I was expecting you to be young, but you seem really young. Do you mind my asking how old you are?" Ryan asked cautiously. He knew it was bad to ask a female her age, but he didn't know if that applied to teenagers.

"I just turned eighteen," she said with a big grin. "This is my first time doing something like this. My dad is trying to help us to learn more about business. I still like dancing and acting, but he doesn't think that it will pay the bills," she laughed.

"Hey, guys," Paul yelled as he walked up to the three of them in their small circle of conversation.

"Hey, Paul," Mike said. "I know you have met Ryan, so I want to introduce Chris. She is Howard's daughter and officially an adult; she just turned eighteen."

"Great," Paul exclaimed. "Happy belated birthday!"

"Thank you … it was just yesterday," Chris said. Neither Ryan nor Mike had picked up on the fact that Chris had just had a birthday, and now Ryan felt silly that he hadn't wished her happiness for the day of her birth.

"Where do you live, Chris?" Paul asked.

"Oh, I live in Georgia right now, but I'm planning to move back here to Detroit, once the projects are underway," she said.

"Great. Well, are we all ready to go meet the president of Trixlar Partners?" Mike asked.

"Yes, sir!" Chris said, laughing.

After their initial meet-and-greet, they all took a van to Randy's office. Ryan was surprised to see how rundown most of the city seemed. The streets were dirty and in poor repair, and there was graffiti on most of the buildings. There were also a lot of homeless people sleeping on the sidewalks. It was amazing to Ryan that this was actually a city in the United States. He had no idea how bad things were in Detroit. He thought that this would be a great place to build one of their first dwellings for veterans. Finally, after driving through the heavy traffic on the litter-strewn streets, they pulled up to the Trixlar Partners office. It was a red brick office in an older row home, with two wooden steps that led to a small porch and a metal door with peeling black paint. Randy greeted them at the door and showed them into his office. He was a dark-haired, good-looking fifty-two-year-old man in good shape. He wore a black suit with black shirt and burgundy tie. His shoes were shiny black leather. He looked out of place, standing in the doorway of the building.

"Sorry for having to meet you here at my old office. Our new office is on the other side of town. It's a little bit more modern. We are in the process of moving," Randy said with slight embarrassment. "Come, have a seat." They all sat around a small round conference table in his office. "By the way, Ben should be arriving soon to give you a tour of the projects we are hoping for Howard and his company to fund."

"Oh, great," said Mike. He was the one who was most familiar with Randy and his business partner's ventures.

Chris smiled a big smile and said, "We are very excited to be here today. Thank you for taking the time to meet with us."

"Absolutely, Chris, I can see you are Howard's daughter. It's great that he has you learning about business at such a young age."

Chris smiled and maintained her composure.

Randy continued. "Now that I have you here, I was hoping you could fill me in on some of the details of Howard's plan, Mike, on building the multifamily dwellings. We have several property owners who have a limited amount of time left to do something with the properties they are holding before they lose them. Howard has guaranteed the financing for them within sixty days. Hopefully, today you can see all of them."

"Sure," Mike said and then broke into a discussion of the financing plan for the Trixlar projects. "We are just waiting for a few of the other financial pieces to fall into place ... It should only be a matter of a couple of more weeks."

Ryan and Paul mostly listened to Mike and nodded in agreement. They both were hearing the financial plan for the first time as well. It sounded like a good plan to them. At one point, Chris pulled out her notebook to double-check something Mike had said.

"Oh, Mike," she interrupted, "I think you meant to say that Adam was going to be able to raise 250 million dollars, not fifty million, for their projects."

"Oh, yes, you are correct, Chris. I meant 250 million dollars," Mike said proudly. *Being able to provide more money, not less, is a mistake I don't mind admitting*, he thought.

"Well," said Randy, "I see that Ben is pulling up out front. Let's go ahead and meet him outside. I've got to go to the airport myself. It was great meeting you guys. I look forward to working with you." Randy stood up and led them out to Ben's van.

After the tour of Detroit and the various projects, Mike, Paul, Ryan, and Chris said good-bye to Ben as he dropped them off at their hotel. They had a full schedule the following day to see the companies. They were going to visit a trucking company called L & S Materials, as well as a glass and a lumber supply company. Ryan's newly formed LLC, Ryan Carroll Construction Company, was going to be the purchaser of the companies, and Ryan was hoping that Mike would be able to help him with how to present himself to the sellers. This was foreign to him for the most part, with the exception of the small amount of experience he had gained from the Miami trip.

The meetings with the sellers of the construction companies went without a hitch. Mike spoke with the sellers, with whom he had spoken by phone on several occasions. There were not a lot of questions. Mike had asked for the financials for each business, and they all had received a copy of their current financials from their respective accountants. All the sellers were excited to show their facilities to them, as well as to their brokers. One broker, named Bo, from L & S Material, seemed especially interested in how the business was going to be purchased. He had additional questions about the structure of the financing. Mike tried to explain it to him but eventually gave up and said he needed to have a discussion with Mr. Holland about it. It had been a long day, and Ryan was looking forward to getting back home to Laura. Mike said he would talk with Howard when he returned and would schedule a follow-up conference call.

The following week, Laura's larger loan closed, and she was able to use some of the funds to make their monthly payments to Ryan's credit cards and loan, as well as Laura's. Other than that, they hadn't heard much from Howard. She texted Howard several times before he finally responded that they were still working with the lawyers to draw up the contracts on the purchase of the medical companies. Mike kept her in the loop by forwarding e-mails to her from the brokers from the medical companies and the construction companies. She also was able to see the e-mail exchange between Adam, Howard, and Mike. They seemed busy, trying to get the applications together for the equipment loans on the medical companies. The issue seemed to be, though, that Laura didn't exactly own the companies yet, so how could she apply for a loan for the equipment? The lending company had valid concerns about this, Laura thought, and Howard told her that he was going to assign a few assets to her company to make it worth more for the sake of purchasing the companies. One in particular was a twenty-million-dollar property called the Salvadore Building in downtown Detroit. Howard said it was owned by his family's trust, but he would temporarily assign it to her business.

After a few weeks, Howard scheduled a conference call with the owners of the medical companies and their respective brokers and lawyers. He told

Laura she could join the call if she wanted, and she decided it would be an interesting lesson for her; she especially wanted to know the precise date of the closings. At the scheduled time, Laura called Howard's number and he silently added her to the conversation. She didn't speak, as Howard was currently speaking in a commandeering voice.

"I am acting as Dr. Carroll's chief financial officer today. I could care less that some of you are not happy with the length of time we need for the closing, or that you have to fill out applications for equipment loans. What it comes down to is this: Do you want to sell you companies or not?" Laura realized that Howard had asked for sixty additional days to close. One of the lawyers for Miami Imaging was not happy with Howard's explanation of the financing either.

"What kind of financing are you talking about here? This is certainly not conventional. Do you even know what you are doing?" Max said. This caused Howard to lose all sense of decorum.

"Look, buddy, you're lucky I'm not there in person. I'm surprised your clients are even using you for this transaction. You seem to be very dense when it comes to financing. Stop wasting my time. I'm about to just move on. I'm doing you all a favor. You know your companies aren't as valuable as you've stated. If you can't get your acts together, I know fifty other companies who can!" Laura cringed as she heard Howard yell. She did not like what she was hearing. John Rogers spoke up and tried to calm Howard down.

"No Howard, it's fine. I'm sorry for Max's comments. He's just trying to protect us. I'll talk to him later." John's business partners were not happy with him at that point and began to pressure John that it was his decision and that if this didn't work out his job was on the line. By the end of thirty minutes, everyone was still on board, at least temporarily. Laura was just glad the call was over, and felt her muscles relax all at once. After the call, Howard only had one comment.

"Laura, I'm sorry you had to witness that. Sometimes I have to play hardball."

A few days later, Howard asked for a conference call with Laura, Ryan, Mike, Paul, and his daughters.

"Hello, everyone," Howard said. "I wanted to give you all an update on the purchase of the companies. Bo, the broker for L&S Materials, wants us to put an additional twenty thousand dollars in escrow for the purchase of their company. I'm not sure I want to do that. He's being a little bit difficult to work with. I am not getting the requested documents from him on his financials. He is exhibiting a major lack of understanding about how I am structuring the financing. What are your thoughts, Ryan? Do you think we should put the money in escrow?"

"Umm … I actually really liked the owners of L&S Materials. It seems to be a solid company. It would really be a good one to purchase," Ryan replied.

"I agree," said Mike. "We can talk to the owner, Thomas, and bypass Bo if we have any other issues with him. Thomas seems to be a reasonable man."

"Okay, then. We will go ahead and put up the escrow. Laura, I'm going to have you send the money from your loan proceeds to L&S Materials today. But I want you to send it to Chris so she can make the payment." Something told Laura that Howard had been planning to pay the escrow, and just wanted to ask their opinions to make them feel like they had a say. She didn't really like the idea of putting money into this company when they already had put the forty thousand dollars down for the Gate Steele company.

"Okay, Chris … how do you spell your last name?" Laura asked.

"S-C-O-T-T, just like the toilet tissue," Chris replied. A couple of people laughed, but Chris didn't seem to think it was that funny.

Laura stopped laughing and remembered the forty thousand dollars. "Howard, what's going to happen to the forty thousand dollars we put down on Gate Steele?" she asked.

"Good question, Laura. We are working with the lawyers to make sure we get that back."

There's no way they would lose that forty thousand dollars, Laura thought. *Howard is too good of a business man to let that happen.* Then again, she didn't know the details of the deal.

CHAPTER 19

Praise the Lord, you His angels, you mighty ones
who do His bidding, who obey His word.
—Psalm 103:20

ON SATURDAY, A WEEK LATER, Ryan and Laura went for their nightly walk with their dog Boo.

"Well, I haven't heard from Howard lately. I texted him several times but no response," Laura said. "Paul actually called me to ask how things were going. I thought he had been kept in the loop, but apparently, he hasn't heard much from Howard either. He said that he only got a couple of texts asking him to find more credit partners. I don't know if that's good news or bad news."

"I'm starting to wonder if getting involved in this was a good idea. At first I thought that we were perfect for this, but now I'm wondering if the people who didn't sign up were being the wise ones. I mean, we were under the impression that they were about to purchase Gate Steele and would be getting salaries and company cars, and so far, we haven't gotten anything but more debt. I'm going to try calling him myself," Ryan said.

"Yeah, I need to ask Howard about the company cars. Our vehicle is so old. We can't even use our credit to buy a car ourselves right now due to borrowing that money for Howard."

"Laura, I think it's time to find a church," Ryan said.

"Oh, I forgot to tell you. A while ago, right before we got involved in this, I watched a sermon on TV by a pastor who was in Dallas. I think we should try his church. I know it's quite a drive, but there really isn't a church around here that I want to attend."

"I'm game," said Ryan. "We can go tomorrow."

After they got back to the house, Ryan called Howard. He didn't answer. Ryan then texted Howard that they needed to talk. He finally got a text from Howard: "Hi Ryan. I'll call you in an hour." The rest of the night went by with no word from Howard.

The next day, Laura and Ryan got up and drove an hour to Gateway Church. Laura knew from watching Pastor Morris on television that he traveled a lot, but she was hoping he would be there that day.

As soon as they walked into the sanctuary, Ryan turned to Laura and said with surprise, "This is the church in my dream!"

"Wow, Ryan, that's awesome. I guess we're in the right place after all," Laura responded.

After the worship band left the stage, Pastor Morris walked out on the stage. He was preaching a series called the Blessed Life. On this particular day, the sermon was called "Breaking the Spirit of Mammon."

"As it says in the book of Matthew, 'no man is able to serve two masters, for either he will hate the one and love the other, or else he will be loyal to the one and despise the other'. Mammon, or love of money, is a spirit, or demon. People who lose money or their jobs may get mad and blame God. Mammon is a jealous spirit and it tries to take the place of God. It promises us everything that only God can give us, like security, freedom, happiness, and respect."

Laura hadn't really thought about this very deeply before, but she listened intently. She started to feel uneasy in her spirit as she realized that perhaps all of this time she had been more concerned about money than God. She had been looking to money as her security. And so far, it hadn't worked out very well. Mammon was producing exactly the opposite of what it promised. She realized that she had had more faith in Stan Powers than Jesus Christ. An overwhelming sense of guilt immediately overtook her.

On the way home after the service, Ryan and Laura had a lot to talk about.

"Laura, I think we have been putting our faith in the wrong things," Ryan said.

"Yes, I feel guilty for thinking that money was the answer. I was so greedy. I have to admit that. I can say that I wanted to have money just so I could give it away, but if I'm being honest with myself, I can say that I also was dreaming about having a lot of nice things … I'm no better than Stan Powers," she responded.

"Don't feel guilty, Laura. You shouldn't feel condemned by it; that's not what God wants. He does try to convict us in our spirits, though. That's how we change, by taking heed of those convictions and doing something about it."

"It's time to stop focusing just on myself and our problems and start to focus on helping more people. I can't wait to get these deals closed with Howard." As she said Howard's name, she felt an explosion from behind her that caused her head to jolt forward. The back wheels of the car swerved to the right and the tires made a screeching sound as Ryan tried to straighten the car. Before she knew it, they were on the side of the highway with both airbags deployed. She was in shock for a few dozen seconds before she heard Ryan's voice. It sounded far away.

"Are you okay, Laura? Laura? Can you hear me?" Ryan put his hand on her shoulder. "Jesus, help us," Ryan pleaded as he continued to pray out loud.

A few minutes later, Laura heard a faint voice. "I'm okay, Ryan," Laura whispered with her eyes still closed. "I'm okay."

Ryan breathed an audible sigh of relief. He opened his car door and got out to see who had hit them from the back. A white Toyota Corolla with a smashed front end was parked about ten yards behind them.

The driver got out of the car while holding his neck. "I'm sorry. I didn't see you. I don't know how I missed you. I've never hit anyone before. Are you okay?" the driver asked with concern.

Ryan saw that the man was walking toward him with an unsteady gait. *Is this guy drunk? Is he staggering from the accident or from drinking?* Ryan thought. *I better keep talking to him.* "I'm okay. I'm just concerned about my wife. But I think she's okay too. I'm trying to find my cell phone to call 911. Do you have a cell phone?" Ryan asked.

"Yeah, let me get it." When the man turned around to walk back to his car, Ryan realized it was in the man's back pocket.

"I think it's in your pocket, sir," Ryan said.

"Oh, right. Uh … my name is Ed," he said as he gave Ryan the phone.

"Thanks." After he called 911, Ryan introduced himself to Ed. He was fairly certain that Ed had some kind of substance in his system, but he couldn't quite tell. He seemed a little off balance but was able to hold a conversation.

"Umm … did you see what I saw earlier?" Ed asked with hesitation.

"I'm not sure what you mean," Ryan replied.

"I almost don't want to say it … you might think I'm hallucinating," Ed said as he scratched his temple and looked down.

"Try me," Ryan prompted.

"It was the strangest thing I've ever seen. I saw a shooting white light and tall … creature, I guess you'd say, wrap itself like a rope of blue light around your car, pick it up, and put it on the side of the road. Then it was gone … just like that." He marveled as he snapped his fingers. "You can say I'm crazy, but I know what I saw."

Ryan stood there in silence, too stunned to speak. Maybe that was why Ed was acting so weird.

The police showed up and then the ambulance came, Laura was loaded into the back of it and taken to the ED in Dallas.

"To be on the safe side, maybe you should go too, Ed," Ryan suggested. He knew that something had happened back there to make their car land where it did. *But was it an angel? I'll have to tell Laura about this … once I make sure she's okay*, he thought.

In the heavenly realm, Willon and Trylon were glad to have gotten free from Wink's trap just in time to save Laura and Ryan from getting seriously injured by the white Toyota. Willon had tried to be discreet. He knew, though, that he decreased his frequency to the point where he could be seen by human eyes. It happened occasionally, and due to the situation, he really didn't have a choice. They had just escaped the firestorm and severed the black webbing that had been holding them. It was Dunamis who had found them and assisted in their release.

"Thank you, Dunamis. I was very concerned that I wouldn't be able to help Laura on time," Willon said.

"It took me longer than I thought to find you. Wink had formed a shield of deception that I wasn't able to get past until now. It was the praying that broke through the deception shield that gave me the power to get to you on time," Dunamis responded. "Then I had to get around Tat and Furies. I know they are currently sending out additional legions of troops to fortify their strongholds, and Chaos and Asm will be among them as well. We will also send for backups. This mission is too important. We cannot underestimate the demonic strategies they will employ. Be on guard at all times," Dunamis commanded with authority. He couldn't put his finger on it, but he had a sense of urgency he had not previously had. He could not know this at the time, but the angels were heading right into Wink's almost perfectly conceived ambush.

After Laura was evaluated in the ED, she was cleared to go.

"I feel like we were just here," she said.

"No kidding," Ryan replied.

On the way home, Ryan asked Laura what she believed about angels. She said she definitely believed they existed; after all, it was in the Bible.

"Yeah, I guess I just never expected that people could see them," he said.

"What do you mean?"

Ryan told her what Ed had related to him at the scene of the accident.

"That's awesome. I just wish I could have seen it," Laura said.

"I thought he was on drugs or something … turns out Ed was just in a state of disbelief. I bet that will change his outlook on things. I know it has changed mine." Ryan laughed.

CHAPTER 20

THE FOLLOWING MONDAY, LAURA RECEIVED an e-mail invitation from Mike to a conference call for "an update with Howard Holland." Laura e-mailed back that they would attend the call and told him about their accident.

"Wow, I'm glad you are both okay," Mike typed.

Later that evening, Laura and Ryan had dinner and got ready for the update. At eight o'clock they signed on to the call. There were eight other people on the call: Laura assumed they were from Eagle Funding Group.

Instead of Howard's usual get-to-the-point attitude, he asked Laura how she was doing. "I heard about your accident yesterday. I hope you and Ryan are both okay," he said with sincerity.

"Oh yes, we are well. But the car is totaled. Which makes it imperative that we get our company cars now. We had to rent a car, and it's the only one we have. It's a good thing my work is so close." She heard someone in the background say he was praying for her full recovery.

"Yes, I'm glad to hear you are well. You guys are like family to us. We definitely want to get those company cars for you. I don't like the idea of your having to rent one. I'll have my daughter Angela continue to work on that. She has been trying to reach someone at a car dealership we have connections with in Georgia. In the meantime, though, I have spent the last week working with the lawyers from the medical company acquisitions. We are looking at a closing date of December 15. In order to move along the Detroit projects, I have had Angela bidding on the Packard Plant. It's a special building in Detroit that used to be an automobile factory for Packard Motor Car Company. Now it's just another ruin. But I believe we can work to resurrect it."

A thought occurred to Laura, and now she reluctantly asked, "Howard, under whose name are you bidding on it?"

"Your business, Laura, but don't worry; it's a confidential auction," he said reassuringly. For some strange reason, she knew he was going to say that. "I'm hoping to spend less than six hundred thousand dollars on it," Howard continued.

"When is the auction over?" she asked.

"Eight days," he answered. "I also want to discuss a new opportunity that has arisen. Mike and I have been working with an investor who has close ties to the United Arab Emirates. His name is Ricky. He will be meeting with them in Hong Kong next month and is going to get funding in the amount of two billion dollars for the Mildred Holland Family Trust. We will be sending representatives from Trixlar Partners, as well as my daughters and Mike. They are requesting that I attend as well. I am still deciding on that. It is a long trip for me, with my health conditions. I'm trying to set up dialysis in Hong Kong. I don't want to let this opportunity slip through our fingers. And Laura, you can go as well, if you would like," Howard said.

"That's okay, Howard. I have to be here to work. Maybe the next trip," she responded regretfully.

The following week, Laura's front office manager buzzed her at her desk to let her know she had a call from a car dealership in Georgia. The caller identified himself as Peter. "I just wanted to make sure that you want the BMWs we have here at the dealership," he said. "Angela Scott called on your behalf, and I just wanted to make sure this was a legitimate request.

"Oh, it is. She is working for my business," Laura replied.

"We will have to run a credit check. Would you like to lease or purchase them?"

Laura didn't know what to say. She needed a car desperately but hadn't realized she would be the one financing them. The more she thought about it, though, the less surprised she was.

"What would be the difference in cost?" she asked.

After going into the details of the lease and the purchase, Laura told Peter she would have to call him back. She wanted to ask Howard about it first. She tried to call Howard, and to her amazement, he answered. She told him the situation, and they decided that it would be best to just lease the vehicles due to the cost. After she hung up the phone, she called Peter back to let him know what she had decided.

"Okay, Dr. Carroll. I'll have the cars delivered to you in the next few days. I'm also going to have our specialist Simon fly out there to show you how to set up the cars. He will be able to walk you through setting up the satellite and also your smartphones. You can also personalize them for your own seat settings and so forth."

Laura hadn't realized that the cars would be so specialized. It would be the first time she would ever drive a brand new car.

The following day was Friday. Laura was looking forward to a Friday night out on the town in Dallas. She and Ryan also were looking forward to getting their new vehicles the following week. As they were walking in downtown Dallas to their new favorite restaurant of Chef Stephan Pyles, Laura's phone rang. She didn't recognize the number so she ignored it.

Just then, Ryan's phone rang as well. "Hello?" he said into his phone, while putting a finger into his other ear. "I can't really understand you. Could you repeat that?" he asked. "Did she what?? No, it was supposed to be six hundred thousand ..." Ryan said.

"Who is it?" Laura asked.

"Some reporter in Detroit," he whispered, covering the speaker.

"Hang up the phone, Ryan. Just hang up!" Laura pleaded.

After Ryan hung up the phone, he said, "Congratulations. You just purchased the Packard Plant for six million dollars."

"*What!?* I thought that was supposed to be a confidential auction ... that's what Howard said." Laura pulled out her phone and called Howard, who didn't answer. Just then, her phone rang and the name Angela flashed on her screen.

"Laura, I have my dad on the line," Angela said. "I was just telling him that I accidentally bid six million on the Packard Plant instead of six hundred thousand. I put one too many zeros."

Laura was getting another call on her phone, and so was Ryan.

"We are getting bombarded by reporters, Howard. I thought you said this was a confidential auction," Laura said in exasperation.

"Don't worry, Laura. We will purchase it. I didn't want to spend so much, but it's okay. I'll have the lawyers call them on Monday morning," Howard said.

"That makes me feel a little bit better," she replied.

The next day, Ryan got a call from his mother, asking if Laura really had bought the Packard Plant. It was in the newspapers. Even Chris called to let her know that her picture was on the news as the buyer of the Packard Plant. Laura had to text her staff over the weekend to let them know they would be hearing something about the Packard plant and to expect some phone calls on Monday morning, in case reporters started calling the office. She got on her Facebook account and saw that she had two hundred new friend requests, all from the Detroit area. She read an article about herself and the conjecture over why she was purchasing the Packard Plant. One person, after seeing that she had photos of her cats on her Facebook page, had guessed that maybe she was buying the Packard Plant to use as a big cat litter box. Laura had laughed at that comment.

Over the weekend, Howard called to let Laura know that he, Mike, and another publicist friend of his were putting together a press release on her behalf as it related to the purchase of the Packard plant. They planned to talk to the city council members on Monday morning to discuss the purchase. Howard said he was going to try to buy some time for the purchase, as the financing had not quite come together.

On Monday morning, Laura went to work as usual, although with more dread. There were twenty-one messages from reporters on the front office answering machine. The calls started pouring in as soon as they turned the phones on. This was definitely the most the phone had rung since she had opened her office. She told her front office manager to just take messages. At lunchtime Chris called her, with Howard on the phone, and she was patched into a conference call with the city council members of Detroit and their lawyers, as well as Mike and the group's recently hired lawyer, Patrick Davis. Laura didn't know Patrick. She thought that Howard's lawyer was a man named Aaron Jones, but Mike had mentioned to her a few days earlier that Aaron had been in a car accident and was not able to participate in their projects. He apparently had broken both of his arms and was unable to write or type. Laura couldn't help but notice that he was the second person in their group to have a car accident.

"Hello, everyone, this is Patrick Davis. I am the lawyer representing Dr. Laura Carroll. She would like to have an additional two weeks to purchase the plant. We have some financing we are obtaining, and we just need a little bit more time."

"Hi, this is Bart Ward. I represent the city. We will have to talk about that. Let's have another call Friday to discuss it."

"We look forward to it," Patrick said.

After everyone from the city hung up, Laura asked Howard what his plan was.

"I think we can talk them into waiting. It is six million dollars, after all—much more than they thought they were going to get for it."

The next morning Howard and Mike's press release came out about their group's plan to remodel the Packard plant and use it for manufacturing prefabricated buildings. *That's not a bad idea,* Laura thought. Unfortunately, though, as she continued to read the article, she felt a sick feeling in the pit of her stomach. Sadly, they hadn't proofread the release very well, and there were bizarre comments about how Detroit had fallen and needed to be cleansed and rebuilt. *This is not good*, she thought. *Why couldn't he stop while he was ahead?*

Howard called Laura on her way to work. She had been getting texts from reporters, asking if she was responsible for the strange press release that had come out overnight. She was dreading the phone calls she expected to get at work.

"Laura, I want you to call the commissioner and then call me, so I can talk to him," Howard requested.

"What do you plan to say, Howard?" she asked.

"I'm just going to follow up on the extension we asked for."

"What happened with that press release?" she asked.

"I think with Mike and so many of us on the call putting it together last night, there was some confusion," he responded.

"I wish someone had asked me to proofread it, Howard. It was very strange and had a lot of mistakes."

"Yeah, I know. You don't have to tell me. I got a call from John at Miami Imaging. Apparently he's from Detroit, and he found out about it. I had to tell him that my daughter accidentally bid the six million on the plant. He thought it was funny, though. I wanted to make sure your reputation wasn't hurt."

"Well, I can only imagine what will be coming out in the news now. So do we have the money for the plant or not?" Laura asked impatiently.

"Yes, but like I said, we will have to wait. It will be up to the commissioner now to see if they will."

"I'll call him now," Laura said. She hung up with Howard and called the commissioner's office.

"Thomas speaking," he said.

"Thomas, this is Dr. Carroll. I would like to discuss our purchase of the Packard plant with you. If you can hold on a second, I'll get Howard, my CFO, on the line." Laura set her phone to dial Howard's number. It rang several times, but he did not pick up. *Come on, Howard. Pick up.* She willed him as hard as she could, but he didn't pick up. "Umm … he's not answering," Laura said with disappointment in her voice.

"If you think you can stall on this, it's not going to work," Thomas said.

"That's not it at all," Laura insisted. "I'll try again later, and we will call you back."

"You have until the end of the day," Thomas said and hung up.

Laura tried calling Howard again, and this time he answered. He seemed oblivious to her frustration.

"What happened, Howard? Why weren't you on the call?" she asked.

"I got rear-ended," he said.

"What? Did you say you got rear-ended? Like, just now?" she asked in disbelief.

"Yes," he responded.

"Are you okay?" she asked.

"Yes, I'm fine. I just finished talking to the guy who hit me. It's over now," Howard said.

Laura couldn't believe the timing. *Now that makes three car accidents,* she thought.

"What happened with the commissioner?" he asked.

"Oh, he wants us to pay by the end of the day," she replied. She was done worrying about it. It was apparent to her that the commissioner wasn't interested in working with their group.

"I'll see what I can do," Howard said unconvincingly.

When she got to her office, she had several messages from reporters.

Her office manager mentioned that a few people had called to see if she was a quack. Also, the CEO of Health for Today stopped by and wanted a word with her. *Great,* she thought. *This will be fun to explain.* She didn't know how this was going to look to her patients. She hoped no one in Jupiter, Texas, other than her employer, would pay attention to the Detroit headlines.

The next day was looking up for Laura. The cars were being delivered that day, and she was excited to get rid of her rental. The driver showed up as scheduled, and Simon got to their house within the same hour. After unloading the vehicles, the driver left. Simon reviewed everything in great detail with Laura and Ryan for each of their cars. It was exciting, and it took their mind off the Packard plant fiasco.

Later that day, Howard called to check in with them and to let them know he was going to have his publicist take care of everything. Laura's company was going to buy a lot of property in Detroit in the near future, and Howard wanted to make sure everyone in Detroit knew it. Laura, on the other hand, was hoping that the people of Detroit would forget she even existed. This had been the greatest embarrassment of her life to date.

In the demonic realm, Tat and Furies were doubled over with laughter. They high-fived themselves until their hands were callused.

"Oh my, what have we done?" Furies said mockingly as tears of laughter poured from his eyes.

"Let's put on our shocked face … Oh no … the horror of it all!" Tat roared again as a new wave of hilarity rose up from within him.

"Har-de-har-har," Wink said sarcastically as he walked in the room, interrupting their gleeful exchange. Tat and Furies tried to compose themselves as quickly as possible.

"I see you are having a wonderful time with your antics, but let's not drop our guard. As fun as this is, there is some serious business ahead of us. I'm sure you understand," Wink reprimanded.

CHAPTER 21

IT WAS THE FIRST WEEK of November, and it was getting close to the Hong Kong trip. Howard wanted to have a conference call to go over everything to make sure they were prepared. Everyone was invited to the call, including the president of Trixlar Partners, Randy Getz, and several of his business partners.

Howard was still reeling from the reprimand he had gotten from his business associate, Adam, over the Packard plant press release. *Have you ever heard of spell check?* Adam had asked. Getting to the point, Howard said, "I have called this meeting today with my secretary, Veronica, on the line. We want to go over the assets of the Mildred Holland Family Trust so everyone is on the same page. Veronica, I'd like you to take notes so you can e-mail everyone with a copy after the call is over."

"No problem, Mr. Holland," Veronica said.

Laura hadn't heard of Veronica before. *She must be his new secretary,* Laura thought.

As Laura listened to Howard, she couldn't help but notice that some of the assets on the list were ones they were trying to purchase but did not own yet. She was feeling confused. One asset in particular was a kaolin mine in Canada. She wasn't sure what kaolin was and quickly Googled it while on the conference call. It turned out to be a clay used in many products, such as cosmetics or even paper products. Mike had told her that Howard was going to purchase the kaolin mine with the proceeds from the UAE loan. Laura took a mental note and planned to ask Mike about this after the call.

Howard continued. "I was supposed to go on this trip as well, as you all are aware, but I started to lose my vision a couple of days ago, and now I have to go for additional testing. I am scheduled for an MRI, and the doctors don't want me to travel at this time. I hope everyone is aware of the gravity of the hour. This is going to be exactly the piece of financing we need to pull everything together."

Howard paused for about fifteen seconds before continuing. *He's trying to make a point,* Laura thought, *and so far, he has.*

After they had a full discussion of the assets, Howard sent a group text to Laura and several others during the call to invite them to a follow-up meeting without Randy or the other associates from Trixlar Partners on the line. Laura agreed.

Soon after hanging up the phone, Chris called her. "Laura, I have my father on the line. We are getting ready to pay you your promissory notes and salary. Please send over all notes that show what Howard has promised you to Chuck Shoeman from Eagle Funding Group so he can get the check ready for you. Once everyone returns from the trip, we should have the financing in a matter of days." Chris paused and her father continued.

"Laura, we will need to use your credit cards to fund the trip. And I'll need you to wire Ricky thirty thousand dollars in exchange for his participation."

Laura did not like hearing that, but she didn't have a choice. She was getting tired of being the only one who supplied the funding. She couldn't wait for Whitney's loan to close. There were supposed to be many more credit partners. But she wasn't going to worry about it at the moment. They were, after all, about to get two billion dollars in financing, and she was excited to finally get paid. Howard had even promised them a bonus.

"Also, while Mike is away, I'm going to need you to do a few things for me," Howard said.

"No problem," Laura said. She wanted to help in any way she could. After all of this time, she didn't want to be the one to slow anything down.

While Mike and Howard's daughters were away in Hong Kong, Laura and Ryan didn't hear very much from anyone. She only then remembered that she meant to ask Mike about the kaolin mine and if the Mildred Holland Family Trust was now the owner of it. She hoped everything was still in order for the closings of the medical companies. Howard had asked her to incorporate a branch of Ryan's construction company in Georgia while Mike was gone. He mentioned that he had been on several conference calls with Ricky and everyone while they were in Hong Kong.

He didn't mention much about the calls and seemed to avoid answering any direct questions from Laura about them. Laura wondered if things were going well, due to Howard's irritable tone.

After a week, Laura got a text from Mike. He had just gotten into the States, and it was midnight there. He sent a picture of Howard, but it had very poor lighting. He said took the photo while in Hong Kong. Ricky had Howard get on Skype for the conference calls so he could see what he looked like. Howard was wearing a baseball cap and had his head down. Laura thought that was odd. For some reason, she just didn't expect Howard to be a baseball cap-wearing kind of guy.

"So how did it go?" she texted back.

"I'll tell you about it tomorrow. I'm wiped out," he replied.

Laura had a hard time sleeping that night and woke up, anticipating a call from Mike. She didn't hear from him all day. By this time, she was beside herself, wondering what the status of the loan was from the UAE. At 6:00 p.m., Laura's phone rang.

"Hi, Laura. How is everything going?" Mike asked.

"I'll give you the answer to that question, Mike, once I find out how things went with you," Laura said impatiently.

"I see. Well, Ricky wants another eighty thousand dollars, and Howard is refusing to give it to him. He said that Ricky is going back on his word. Randy told Howard that he should just give it to him."

"Yeah, but Randy doesn't know that we don't have that much to pay him. Why doesn't Howard just use his own money?"

"At this point, Laura, I'd have to guess that he doesn't have any to give, or he would have closed some of these transactions months ago. Evidently, Chris brought along a friend, Sally, who used to date Howard, and Sally seemed to get along really well with Ricky, if you know what I mean. So Howard is a little bit upset with Sally right now too. He thinks she may ruin things for us. Ricky told Sally that he doesn't think Howard has the money to pay him."

Laura cringed.

"This is starting to sound like a soap opera, Mike," an exasperated Laura complained.

"Yep, it is. But don't say anything to Howard about it. He doesn't want you guys to know," Mike requested.

"No problem; just keep me in the loop, please. What is the next step now? Oh, I almost forgot—I was going to ask you this before you went to Hong Kong. Does the Mildred Holland Family Trust now own the kaolin mine?"

"No, that's the other problem. I think Sally knew that and told Ricky. Evidently, Ricky has a business partner who was working with Howard on some financing and is still waiting for Howard to come through for him as well," Mike said. "He is a movie producer who was looking for funding for one of his new movies. Maybe you've heard of him? His name is Spade Samuelson."

"His name sounds vaguely familiar. I'll have to Google him," Laura said.

"Anyway, I think Ricky partly went to Hong Kong to try to get more information about Howard in case Spade decides to sue him," Mike said.

"That's not good news," Laura said. She started to feel a spasm in the back of her neck.

"Nope."

"I'm starting to get really nervous, Mike. We don't have any money left on our credit cards, and the loan money is all gone. We have a large sum of money to pay this month, and no money to pay it. Now it's starting to look like the UAE loan isn't even going to happen."

"I didn't realize how tight things were with the payments. I wish I had known sooner. A few weeks before we left for Hong Kong, Howard had asked me if I knew anyone who would be a credit partner, and I signed up my mom and dad. They are on a fixed income right now but have great credit. He had them borrow a hundred thousand dollars. He promised to pay them back double by January. Now I'm starting to get worried. I sent all of the loan proceeds to his daughter Whitney. Well, I'm going to keep doing my job until we can get one of these deals closed. I have a lot at stake … and I haven't been paid anything yet for all of my work."

Laura was starting to realize she wasn't going to get any sympathy from Mike.

The next morning, Mike called Laura at eight o'clock.

"Good morning, Mike. How are you?" Laura asked cheerfully. She had woken up after having a pleasant dream about taking a trip to Hawaii with Ryan to celebrate their anniversary. She was still thinking about it when the phone rang.

"Not so good, Laura. Just standing here on a stool with my neck inside a noose, trying to decide if I should jump off the stool," Mike said.

"What?" she said abruptly. As she was thinking of what to say next, with the mental image forming in her mind, Mike interrupted.

"Figuratively speaking, of course," he added, a little too slowly for Laura's liking.

She wasn't looking forward to the answer as she asked, "Why? What's wrong?"

In his charming Southern drawl, he replied, "I don't believe it could get any worse, my dear. Mr. Holland has been in a car accident and apparently is in the hospital with a broken jaw and not able to use his right arm. I think Whitney said he might have had a stroke. Who knows if the stroke caused the car accident, or car accident caused the stroke. It seems touch-and-go right now. But he's not able to communicate with anyone. Whitney got a call from a nurse at the hospital. That's all I know."

"That's terrible. Which hospital is it?" Laura asked.

"I don't know any of the details yet," Mike replied. "I'll be speaking to Whitney soon, I'm sure. She texted me that she and Chris are going to drive to visit him since all of our credit cards are maxed out, and they can't schedule flights."

"Wow, I hope he's okay," Laura lamented. She was starting to get really nervous, not knowing the status of Howard's health or any of the transactions.

"I'll let you know as soon as I find out anything," Mike said before Laura could ask any more questions.

What are we going to do if Howard is out of commission? Laura thought. She went to find Ryan to let him know the bad news.

"Hey, Ryan, let's go for a walk," she suggested as she rounded the corner to the shop in the backyard.

"Okay, just give me a minute," he said. As he looked at her, he immediately knew something was very wrong.

"We better start praying for Howard," she said.

"Why? What happened?" Ryan asked anxiously as he grabbed his baseball cap and put it on his head, anticipating the strong morning rays of sunshine. They walked out of the shop and headed toward the front yard to do their usual two-mile walk.

"Howard was in a car accident," Laura said. "I'm not sure if he had a stroke first or after the accident, but I guess it was bad. He isn't able to talk due to a broken jaw and isn't able to use his right arm. Whitney and Chris are headed there to see what's going on. It's a long drive, and they can't fly because we are maxed out on the credit cards. This is so terrible."

"Wow, I don't even know what to say. It absolutely stinks. Here it is, the holiday season, almost Christmas, and we basically have no money and no way to know what's going on with Howard. How did we ever get to this position? We've got hundreds of thousands of dollars of debt and a couple of stupid promissory notes. We haven't even closed a deal, and it's almost been a year! I've had it. I have no idea what to do now. We can't pay our credit card or loan payments. We can't even afford our car payments for two overpriced cars we didn't even need," Ryan finished with a desperate sigh.

"I know. We can't do anything but wait to hear from Whitney and Mike."

They walked in silence for a few minutes, each contemplating a different disastrous ending to their involvement with Howard Holland.

Ryan broke the silence. "Well, in order to make our payments and keep our good credit, I'm going to have to sell my equipment—my tractor and my tow truck. I have no choice."

"Let's see what happens first, after Whitney arrives at the hospital to see Howard. It should only be a few days," Laura said.

"I guess that makes sense," Ryan replied. "I wish we'd never gotten involved in the first place. Things just haven't gone as planned from day one. Even your business is hurting. We can't afford to stay here; we don't even have any income. What a way to celebrate the new year."

"I know, babe; it's time to start praying," Laura said.

In the demonic realm, Furies smiled with pride as he pondered his accomplishments to date. Things were working out so well. His plan was unfolding seamlessly. He had to give himself a pat on the back for hatching such a grand scheme. But as the cliché goes, he was just getting started. He had no intention of letting Tat get the credit for his plan. He wanted the glory all for himself. When he heard Ryan talk about praying more, he became irate. He decided, although he was probably—no, *definitely*—the most scheming of all demons, that having to recruit a little bit of help wouldn't hurt his reputation, as long as they knew their place.

About a week later, Laura still hadn't heard anything from Mike or Whitney so she decided to call Adam. Adam answered on the third ring. In a shaky voice, Laura said, "Hi Adam, this is Laura Carroll. How are you?"

"Oh, hi Laura," he responded.

"Sorry to bother you. I was just wondering if you knew what was going on with Howard or any of our deals?"

"No, I was hoping you were going to fill me in," he replied.

At that point Laura couldn't help it—with all of the stress and the fear of losing everything, she broke down in tears. She tried to hide it and continued the conversation in between silent sobs. "I don't know what we are going to do. We have to pay about seven thousand dollars a month in our debt payments alone, let alone having money to live on."

"I'm sorry to hear that, Laura. I'm not sure why we haven't closed a deal yet. I'm waiting to get paid for my work. I've brought Howard many, many businesses and lenders as well. I know the entire plan from start to finish. I'm just waiting to hear something, just like you are," Adam said with frustration in his voice.

"Well, if you hear anything, let me know, and I'll do the same," she said.

"Will do, Laura," Adam said as he hung up the phone.

While Laura and Ryan were waiting for any news about Howard, Ryan put his tow truck and tractor up for sale. It didn't take long for both of them to sell. Laura wasn't sure what to do about future monthly payments on her loans and credit cards, and she was starting to fret about it all day, every day. She texted Whitney and Chris but was unable to get a response. Finally, about two weeks later, she got a call from Mike.

"I have an update for you," he said.

"Good. What's going on?"

"Well, Whitney has been there at the hospital, waiting for Howard to regain consciousness, and he finally did a few days ago. Chris had to leave, but Whitney stayed behind to be Howard's eyes and ears … and his voice. It sounds like he had a stroke and is trying to learn to use his right arm and speak again. His jaw was wired shut due to the fracture, and he wasn't able to talk at all. But now he is able to move his jaw, although the speech is still slow. He is feeling frustrated. He started doing conference calls again yesterday, and I was on one with him. Whitney had to do most of the talking for him."

"How long do you think he will be in the hospital?" Laura asked.

"I don't know, but I know that he will be doing inpatient physical therapy," he said.

"Well, at least he's okay. What conference call were you on yesterday?" she asked.

"We were talking to a group of people in the Bahamas. It's another deal Howard has been working on for a while," Mike said.

Laura couldn't believe Howard was working on yet another deal as well as everything else they had going on. "What's going on with the UAE loan?" Laura asked tentatively. She couldn't help but ask questions since she had Mike on the phone and wasn't sure when she would get another chance.

"Well, we are having a conference call with Trixlar Partners about that tomorrow night, both Randy Getz and his right-hand man, Carl Shearer, so we will see," Mike replied.

Chapter 22

LAURA WOKE UP EARLY THE next day, even though it was her day off. Ryan was already awake and in the kitchen, making coffee.

She got up and walked into the kitchen. "Good morning, Ryan. How did you sleep?" she asked as she gave him a hug and kiss on the cheek.

"Pretty good. I had this crazy nightmare that we lived in the middle of nowhere, and we borrowed several hundred thousand dollars to buy companies with an almost complete stranger who became incapacitated in a rehabilitation facility, and we weren't able to pay our bills," he said with a straight face.

Laura smirked. "Good one, but unfortunately that wasn't a nightmare; it's our sad reality," she said regretfully.

"Oh, but it's still a nightmare … even while awake, it still qualifies."

"Yeah, I wish someone could pinch us, and we could wake up, and this whole thing would be over. Hopefully, things will turn around now that Howard's health is improving. I mean, could it get any worse?"

"I wish you hadn't said that …"

After having coffee, Ryan went out to the shop to sand the hood of a 1963 Jaguar. He enjoyed doing bodywork, and it helped to keep his mind off their dire situation. Laura got dressed and sat down at the computer to see if she had any new word from Mike or anyone involved in the deals. As she looked at her e-mail in-box, she noticed an e-mail forwarded from Mike and a second copy sent directly from Spade Samuelson, the movie producer. She couldn't help but notice the subject line, which was all in capital letters: TO ALL WHO HAVE INVESTED TIME AND/OR MONEY WITH HOWARD HOLLAND.

She suddenly got a queasy feeling in the pit of her stomach, and her

131

heart skipped a beat. She hesitated before opening the e-mail and then took a deep breath and double clicked on it. It appeared to be a letter to Howard with many attachments and looked like it had been sent to everyone involved in the transactions from Eagle Funding, as well as Howard and his daughters, Mike, Paul, Ricky, and Trixlar Partners, as well as Laura and Ryan. It read:

Hello all,

I have attached some communications that I had with Mr. Howard Holland over the last year. It appears that his so-called company, "Eagle Funding Group," has promised financing for my upcoming movie sequel. I would like to share with you some e-mails that you may find interesting. I plan on exposing all of you who have involvement. And Howard Holland, if that's his real name, is going to pay big time. With my connections, you will see your faces all over the Internet; I can promise you that. I want either the financing I was promised or one hundred thousand dollars in damages for losses to my film company due to your empty promises. Have a lovely day.

Sincerely,
Spade Samuelson

See attachments.

Laura scrolled through the e-mails and saw a picture attached at the end with most of their faces and names and the word FRAUD written over it in big red letters. She was not sure what to think. She knew Howard had been working on other projects, but she certainly didn't want to be considered a fraud. If anything, she was a victim, just like Spade, with all of the empty promises. She started to look at the e-mails. They went from oldest to newest, starting almost one year earlier. She scanned through some of the e-mails in a cursory fashion in order to get the gist of the past year's conversations between Howard and Spade.

Hello, Mr. Holland,

It was a pleasure speaking with you the other day. I look forward to working with you on the financing for my new film, *Blue Dragon: The Sequel*. Please provide the commitment letter for the one hundred million dollars from Eagle Funding Group.

Thank you,
Spade

The next e-mail was dated two weeks later:

Hello, Mr. Samuelson,

The pleasure was mine. I will send the one hundred million dollar commitment letter from my company, Eagle Funding Group, immediately. As you know, I am in the process of wrapping up the financing on several other projects with my family trust, Mildred Howard Family Trust.

Howard

And then, four weeks later:

Hello, Howard,

It's been several weeks since we last spoke. I am still waiting for the commitment letter. I hope you are well. When can we speak again?

Spade

Two weeks later:

Hello, Spade,

I have been having some small delays with the financing for my family's other projects. Please be assured that things are still on track. I will be available for a conference call with my assistant Sally tomorrow at 5:00 p.m. eastern time.

Howard

The next day:

Hello, Howard,

I did not hear from you yesterday. I tried to call you at 5:00 on the dot but didn't get a response. I have put other financing on hold in order to obtain it from your company. Please let me know the status.

Spade

Two days later:

Hello, Spade,

I am sorry for the delay. I have wrapped up my other financing and have submitted to you the one hundred million dollar commitment letter. I will have you submit the one hundred thousand dollar funding fee at your convenience. I will have my assistant Sally call you with instructions for submission of the fee.

Howard

Hello, Mr. Samuelson,

I have been instructed by Mr. Howard to contact you with payment instructions. After reviewing your application, we have decided to fund your film *Blue Dragon: The Sequel*. Welcome to the Eagle Funding family. Please submit the fee per the attached instructions.

Sally

Laura continued to scroll through the e-mails and got to the e-mails from two weeks earlier:

Howard,

I sent the money months ago, and I haven't gotten my funding. Ricky and your ex-assistant Sally tell me that she used to be your girlfriend and that you and your "family trust" is just a scam, that it has no assets. Why is it that I can't seem to find out anything about your family? If you don't give me the funding, you will be sued, and I will expose you and your cohorts.

Spade

Spade,

Relax, Spade. You will get your funding. I don't appreciate the accusations or the subversive way you tried to outmaneuver me to learn about my family's assets by using Ricky under the guise of obtaining funding from the UAE. (And tell me why I shouldn't sue you?) I personally guarantee that you will get your funding. It is taking longer than expected to obtain the larger sums of money, but everything is still in the works.

Howard

Finally, Laura read the last e-mail:

Howard,

When?

Spade

Laura could tell from the e-mails that Howard had strung poor Spade along like he had strung them along. Now she just needed to talk to Mike about this. She was definitely worried about how this would reflect on them. Laura decided to give Mike a call. Just as she was dialing his number, Mike called her.

"I take it you read the e-mails?" Mike asked.

"Oh yes, it was grrreeaatt," she said slowly and with as much sarcasm as she could muster. "I especially liked seeing my face with the work 'fraud' written over it."

"Don't worry, Laura. Spade can't do anything. Howard has already called him to let him know he'll be getting sued himself if he tries to publish any of that stuff about us," Mike said.

"What about Trixlar Partners?" she asked.

"They are a little hesitant now, but Randy is still asking that Howard pay Ricky the money to get the funding, and Randy is now also demanding that he and his partner take over the decision making about the closings for the Detroit companies, since they are on the ground there. Randy knew there was something not right about Ricky when we were in Hong Kong, and then he did a Google search and found that he owned some kind of massage parlor in Australia. So that guy is pretty shady to begin with. But we have that conference call tonight, and Randy thinks he will be able to patch things up with Ricky and even Spade…and don't forget, we also have the Bahamas deal in the works."

Laura was slowly getting a headache, and it was only nine in the morning. She was wishing, like Ryan, that she hadn't asked if it could get any worse. *The dumbest question ever asked,* she thought as she rubbed the bridge of her nose with her thumb and forefinger.

"Sounds like a pretty big mess to me," Laura said.

"Unfortunately, we both have a vested interest in all of this working out," Mike said.

"Yeah, and every day it seems like it's getting less and less likely," Laura replied.

"I'd like to keep a positive attitude about it," Mike reprimanded.

"So would I, if it were possible. See you later, Mike. Just let me know how the conference call goes," Laura responded.

"No problem. I'm taping them now, so I'll just send you a recording," Mike said.

"Even better," Laura said. Deep down, she wasn't sure how much of this she could take. It seemed like a big disaster. She knew she had to go tell Ryan the latest news.

Wink was in his study, having an impromptu meeting at his large round conference table with two of his 65th Battalion officers, Tat and Furies. Since Laura and Ryan had moved to Jupiter, the demons had steadily been waging as many skirmishes as possible, and so far they had been winning. As newly appointed officers, Tat and Furies had both been awarded twelve inches of height since that time and carried themselves much more pridefully than in the past. They were voting today on a promotion for their colleagues Asm, Chaos, and Solum, who had recently been temporarily transferred to Jupiter and the 65th Battalion due to a request by Wink. Wink had been especially impressed by Solum and had seen his ability to pervade the soul of Stan Powers, and he was hoping that he could have the same effect on Laura's and Ryan's souls. Wink had an underlying suspicion, of course, that somehow Solum might try to take his place as the commander, and he couldn't help but be a little bit jealous of him. *I better watch him closely,* he thought.

"The two of you have been working diligently in the Jupiter matter with those two despicable creatures, Laura and Ryan. It has been wonderful to watch," Wink remarked thoughtfully.

"Tat and I were just saying the other day what a genius scheme we have orchestrated so far, especially your suggestion, Wink, to prey on their greedy natures." Furies crowed as he put his slippery scaly "hands" behind his head as to recline in his chair. He knew all of the credit truly belonged to him, but he was a devout sycophant.

"As I see how this is unfolding, I cannot help but be pleased with our progress. But today, nevertheless, we have no time for back-patting or excessive flattery. We must stay vigilant and continue our plan as scheduled. The angels seem to be ten steps behind, as usual. The poor … things. They really don't know how dire their situation is. I have a feeling, though, that once they see Solum and our other two transfers, they will start to catch on." Wink grinned unnaturally before continuing. "Speaking of whom, we do have to decide today if Chaos, Asm, and Solum should be promoted," Wink said.

Tat and Furies nodded.

"First of all, I want you both to know that I would never promote them above you. I have a feeling you might have felt a little bit threatened," Wink said while looking them both in the eyes.

Wink was lying, of course, about not promoting them above Tat and Furies. He knew that all three of them had the potential to grow taller than Tat or Furies. And if that happened, they would be inevitably granted promotion again, and Wink would be happy to grant it. Speaking his intuition about Tat and Furies feeling threatened was a calculated manipulation to turn the discussion and to make them both become defensive and deny their true feelings. And it worked. Tat and Furies both were thinking the same thing: *Hellooo … of course I feel threatened!* But since Wink basically was accusing them of it, they had to deny it vehemently and, in the process, vote for their promotions, even though it was the last thing they wanted.

"Wink, I'm surprised that you think so lowly of us. Of course, we want them to be promoted," Tat insisted. He looked at Furies, who was nodding his head in agreement. "Right, Furies?"

"Yes, I insist on it," Furies said emphatically.

"Then I think it's settled. Let's call them in and give them the excellent news," Wink exclaimed.

After they gave their newly promoted combat soldiers the news, they sat down to discuss and exchange strategies about their best course of action moving forward. Wink spoke with Solum at length about the importance of his role. Their plans had been working even better than expected, but they discussed all possible outcomes at length to make sure they wouldn't be taken off guard. As far as they could tell, their plan was foolproof.

Solum was ready.

CHAPTER *23*

AFTER THE CALL WITH MIKE, Laura went out to the shop to find Ryan. She took Boo and Mollie, the border collie, with her.

"Hey, Ryan. I got some interesting e-mails this morning. Would you like me to tell you about them?" Laura said. She knew the quicker she could have this conversation, the better.

"Whoa, slow down. What are you talking about?" Ryan said.

"Oh, you know. Remember that silly comment I made earlier—'Could it get any worse?'" She asked with a wrinkled nose and pursed lips.

"Oh yes, I remember … when I said 'I wish you hadn't said that'? Let me guess … um, yes, it can get worse, and … it already has?" He hoped he was wrong but feared he was right.

"How did you know?" she said, feigning surprise. Laura then explained the e-mails and the threats from Spade Samuelson. And the subsequent call with Mike.

"Well, I'm surprisingly not surprised!" Ryan said. "I guess you can just keep me posted. There's absolutely nothing we can do."

"I guess we could pray for these deals to still close," she replied.

"Yeah, I think we need to stop thinking of prayer as a last resort," Ryan said.

"Good point, Ryan," Laura said.

Laura, Boo, and Mollie walked back into the house, and Laura went into the kitchen to make a late breakfast. She turned on the television to see what she could find to watch that might raise her spirits while she made lemon blueberry waffles. She was hoping to find a good cooking channel, but she ended up turning to a show where a female preacher was talking about faith.

"You've got to speak out what you believe, not what the enemy believes. Fear is the opposite of faith. Your words are powerful. They have the power to affect your future. You cannot go around expecting bad things to happen because they will. You have to have expectation for good things if you want good things to happen. You can have faith, but you have to actually use it, or it's just like not having any," the preacher said.

Laura agreed with that statement. She knew that she hadn't really believed anything good was going to happen. And she definitely was scared—scared of losing everything and having all of the debt to pay back. She felt something within confirming that what she was hearing was true.

The preacher continued. "What God has planned for you is something better than anything you could want for yourself. You have to pray the will of God, not your will. If what you ask for is not right for you, then he won't give it to you. God said, 'You have not because you ask not.' So it's important to ask. And if you don't get it, then God's going to give you something better."

"Sounds good to me," Laura said out loud to the television. After making the waffles, Laura called Ryan to come in to eat.

"Um … *umm* … these are delicious, Laura," Ryan exclaimed as he stuffed a large piece of waffle into his mouth.

"Thanks, babe. I made them from scratch. I tried experimenting a little bit and put a lot of lemon zest in there as well as lemon juice," she replied.

"I can definitely taste the lemon. They taste like your lemon blueberry cheesecake. Are there any more?" Ryan asked as he chomped away on the waffles.

"I think you asked if there were any more," She joked, pretending to decipher his garbled question. "No, but you can have the rest of mine. I'm stuffed," Laura said.

"What are you going to do the rest of the day?" Ryan asked.

"I was hoping we could go to Dallas tonight to go to the movies. There's a new movie that came out yesterday I was hoping to see," Laura said.

"Sure. Would it be a romance, by any chance?" Ryan asked knowingly.

"Maybe," she replied as she smiled.

Laura thought the movie was just okay. As they were driving home from Dallas, Laura's mood changed. She was wondering how they had gotten in the position they were in. It was like a blanket of dread thrown over her head that she couldn't get out from under. Sure, she could keep herself occupied, but there was always a feeling that something bad was going to happen. She couldn't believe all of the stuff they had gone through. She also was still fearful that they might get into another car accident. She tried to stop thinking about it and noticed neither of them had talked for twenty minutes.

"Hey, Ryan, what are you thinking about?" Laura asked.

"Oh, nothing," he responded. "I'm just tired."

That's always what he says when he doesn't feel like talking, she thought. Laura couldn't blame him, though. What was the point? It did no good to complain. After hearing that female preacher on the TV, she was trying to at least start *thinking* about what she was thinking about and speak only positive things out loud.

They pulled into their driveway at 11:15 p.m. As they walked in the door, their dogs greeted them with wagging tails. Boo jumped up, almost landing in Laura's arms. For a small dog, his vertical jump was impressive.

"Well, hello, Boo. I guess you missed me," she said, laughing as she gave him a kiss on the nose. Boo licked her face in return. Laura smiled as she wiped off her face with the back of her hand.

It's good to be home, Laura thought. She was tired, but she was still hoping that Mike might call her or e-mail her the conference call recording.

As she was getting ready for bed, her phone rang from the top of her nightstand. She ran to it and saw that it was Mike.

"Hello?" she said tentatively.

"Hi, Laura. I hope I didn't wake you," Mike said.

"Oh, no. It's actually good timing," she responded.

"Good. I wanted you to know I'm going to send the recording of the call to your e-mail in the morning, but I just wanted to give you an overview of what was discussed," Mike said.

"Okay."

"I was on the call with Trixlar Partners, Ricky, and Howard. Randy Getz asked Howard to explain his family trust in more detail. Howard put up a smoke screen and changed the subject very quickly. He started to tell Ricky how much of a disappointment he was and told him the UAE deal was off. He berated him until Ricky finally just got off the call. Of course, that caused Randy to raise cane. Randy is very concerned that their special projects in Detroit aren't going to be funded. You and I both know that we probably won't have any money in time for funding the projects that Trixlar Partners want to put into play. I think Randy is getting ready to walk away. Howard told him he was working with a group in the Bahamas and with the prime minister to help build infrastructure. Then Howard asked me to go over the projects and funding for the Bahamas deals. I think after I finished going over all of that, everyone felt better. Randy then asked Howard to explain what happened with Spade's funding. He told him he was relying on the UAE loan but that obviously it wasn't going to happen, so Spade would have to wait for the Bahamas deals to close.

"As convoluted as it seems, I think I follow you. It sounds like Howard is back to his old self," Laura said. "So what's the next step?"

"Well, Whitney is going to the Bahamas to meet with a group that has connections with the prime minister to do some projects close to their airport. She is going to represent the Mildred Howard Family Trust. I think she's going a couple of days after Christmas."

It was hard for Laura to believe that Christmas was only a week away. They didn't have any special plans to visit family; they simply couldn't afford it. Laura was lamenting the fact that they didn't even put up a Christmas tree. She decided that they would just stay home and have a turkey. Just as she was thinking about what to get Ryan for Christmas, Ryan walked into the room.

"Who was that on the phone?" he asked.

"Mike. He just wanted to fill me in on the conference call. Sounds like we aren't going to get any funding from the UAE, but I think we'll be okay when it comes to Spade trying to damage our reputation."

"I'm so tired of all of this. Let's just agree to get out of it as soon as we are able," Ryan said.

"I agree wholeheartedly," Laura replied.

The next day was Sunday; they planned to drive to Dallas for church, but when the alarm went off, Ryan pushed the snooze button. He ended up pushing the snooze button three times before Laura got up and just turned off the alarm. It was obvious they weren't going to make it to church on time, so Laura fell back asleep. When they finally got up, they realized there was a Christmas program at church that evening. They decided to drive to the Galleria mall in Dallas for some shopping and dinner before the show. Neither of them could really get into the holiday mood, and they were hoping the Christmas program would uplift their spirits. Laura was feeling guilty about spending any money at all on Christmas presents or going out to dinner, but she pushed the thoughts away.

While at the mall, Laura bought Ryan a nice yet casual G-Shock watch. He had lost his last G-Shock when they moved to Jupiter and had never gotten a new one. She had told Ryan she didn't want anything—except maybe a gift card or two so she could go shopping after Christmas. She knew that was when to get the best deals. After dinner, they drove to the church.

The program was very entertaining. She had heard that Gateway Church always put on a good Christmas program, and it definitely met her expectations. On the way home, Laura and Ryan listened to Christmas music on the radio. When they got home, Laura decided to do some late-night baking and make some sugar cookies. She was determined to make the best of things, even though it was difficult due to their circumstances. Ryan helped Laura decorate the cookies, and they sat down in the kitchen to watch TV and have coffee and cookies. For the time being, life almost seemed normal. As Laura was flipping through the channels, she came across an individual who seemed to be a Christian, who was saying that she prayed Psalm 91 over her family every day. She said it was a psalm of protection. As the woman read through the Psalms, Laura thought maybe they should start doing that as well. It was obvious that they needed some help.

"Ryan, let's start declaring Psalm 91 every day over ourselves, our families, property, and pets," Laura said.

"Sure, maybe we should declare it a couple of times a day," he said emphatically.

The demons Chaos and Asm had been listening to their conversation. They didn't like what they were hearing. The idea of Laura and Ryan declaring God's Word caused them some anxiety.

"We are going to have to stop that right away," Chaos declared.

"Don't worry, Chaos. I can make them forget that by tomorrow. I'll just throw a couple of distractions their way," Asm replied.

On Christmas morning, Ryan and Laura opened their gifts to one another. Ryan was happy with his new watch, and Laura got three different gift cards to her favorite stores. They ate a traditional turkey dinner with mashed potatoes, stuffing, green beans, and sweet potato casserole, prepared by Laura. The rest of the day was quiet for them. They spoke on the phone with their families and went for a walk around their property with the dogs to help burn off the astronomical amount of calories that they had digested. They both laughed as they joked that if they hadn't gone on the walk they would have remained comatose for the rest of the day.

At around 5:30, after the dogs had their special dinner of turkey and mashed potatoes, Laura got ready to take them outside to do their business. She usually put Boo on a leash, since he had a habit of running away and not coming when called, but for some reason she couldn't find it. She asked Ryan to look for it, but he couldn't find it either, courtesy of Asm. *Oh well,* she thought, *it will be okay just this once.*

"Okay, guys, let's go out," Laura said. As soon as she said that, both dogs started wagging their tails, and Boo started to jump up and down. They ran down the hallway to the back door and ran out as soon as Laura flung it open. Unfortunately, Laura hadn't noticed that there was a huge skunk about twenty-five yards away in the front yard, sniffing around in the bushes. By the time Laura saw the skunk, it was too late. Both dogs were running straight for it. As she screamed *Noooo,* she saw a cloud of spray coming from the skunk that stopped both dogs in their tracks. To Laura's dismay, the inevitable had occurred. The skunk ran off, and the dogs tried to chase it farther out into the field in the front yard, but the irritation of the malodorous fog was starting to take effect. The dogs began to run around, then roll in the grass, and then try to slide their bodies through the grass in vain, trying to wipe it off. Laura couldn't help but laugh.

"Ryan, we've got a problem!" Laura yelled from the door.

"What's wrong?" He said as he came to see what was going on.

"Skunk," she said.

Immediately, with that one word, Ryan knew. "Oh no!" As Ryan looked out at the dogs, he started to laugh as they, half-blinded, continued trying to pursue the skunk. "Those *stupids*," he said, still laughing. Which caused Laura to laugh even harder.

They spent the next hour washing the dogs. Laura looked up a recipe online that was supposed to be a no-fail solution to remove all traces of skunk smell. Evidently, the tomato juice remedy was not effective and was more of a myth. The recommended solution contained hydrogen peroxide, baking soda, and dish soap. It worked pretty well, at least, after three applications. Unfortunately, the smell had entered their house by the back door as well. Laura hadn't realized how strong the smell could be. This was a first for her, and she hoped it was the last. They decided to wait for the smell to evaporate from their room, so they spent the rest of the evening in the living room at the front of the house, with the dogs in the garage.

When she got to the office the next day, Laura hoped that she didn't smell like skunk. She had humbly asked her office manager to smell her to see if any tinges of skunk smell remained. The manager assured Laura, under a hidden smile, that it did not. The office was quiet, but the number of refill requests that she received through her electronic medical record system was overwhelming. It seemed that most people assumed that her office was closed for the day, so she didn't have a full schedule. She wasn't expecting to hear anything from Mike but checked her e-mail that morning to see if there was any news about the Bahamas deals. She saw a couple of forwarded e-mails from Mike that were recorded conference calls between a spokesperson of a group called "A Better Bahamas," Mike, Howard, his daughters, and the assistant to the prime minister of the Bahamas. She knew that Howard had been working hard, and it didn't surprise her one bit that he had worked through Christmas. She couldn't wait to get the opportunity to listen to the recordings.

When she got home, she and Ryan ate a nice dinner that he claimed to have slaved over all day. It turned out to be leftover turkey and gravy sandwiches with jellied cranberry sauce. Laura wasn't going to complain; after all, there was nothing better than leftover Christmas dinner.

"Ryan, this meal is phenomenal. I don't know how you do it," she teased.

"I've learned from the best, cutie," he replied and pinched her cheek.

When she told Ryan about the recorded conference calls, he said,

"Go ahead and listen to them, and just let me know if there's anything important said." Laura realized that Ryan had lost all interest in hearing about the deals. He didn't talk to Howard or Mike and only got on conference calls if he was specifically asked to be on them. He was, as he said, "D-O-N-E—done" with it all. Of course, Laura knew that someone had to keep in touch with them in order to get paid.

Laura spent the next two hours listening to the calls. She was impressed that Howard was doing a business transaction with the prime minister of the Bahamas and wondered how that had come about. It sounded like Whitney was going to be in the Bahamas for a meeting with the members of A Better Bahamas and would have a meeting with the prime minister. *Maybe things are looking up after all,* she thought. She had been getting a lot of anxiety since she received those e-mails from Spade Samuelson, and now that the anxiety was lessening, she began worrying about paying her monthly debt. She didn't have enough money to pay all of the credit cards or loans and had to choose which ones to pay. She decided to throw caution to the wind and text Mike: "Hey, Mike, I listened to the conference calls and was wondering if you had any idea when we might close a deal in the Bahamas?"

"Shouldn't be long now," he texted back.

"Just let me know how Whitney's trip goes," she texted

"Of course," he typed back.

Another week went by, and Laura hadn't heard anything from Mike. Both Laura and Ryan were feeling the stress of all of the debt load they had acquired and the lack of money coming in to cover it. With all of the anxious thoughts in their minds, neither Laura nor Mike remembered their plan to pray Psalm 91. Ryan was also having anxiety about not doing tree work or bringing in money for them to help cover the bills. Laura was beside herself over not hearing anything from Mike or Howard. Again, several texts had gone unanswered. When she continued to get no response, she surmised that it usually was a bad sign. In Laura's frustration, she texted Chris as well to let her know she needed money to pay her debt. Chris's only response was that everything would be fine and that her family had no intention of letting anything bad happen to her credit. Laura replied that it already had.

The following month went by very slowly, and other than a few e-mails forwarded from Mike, there was nothing new. As she was reading through her e-mail, the phone rang.

"Hi, Laura, this is Paul."

"Oh, hey, Paul, it's been a while," she said. Laura hadn't had many conversations with Paul since she became a credit partner and was curious to see if he had heard anything from Howard.

"I was calling because I got a call from Howard, and he asked me to have a meeting here in Olympia to get more credit partners. I'm confused because I didn't think we needed any," Paul said.

"Yeah, that is kind of weird." In her mind, though, she knew things weren't going well, and this was only more evidence to support her case.

"I thought things were going well. Mike texted me the other day to let me know it wouldn't be long before we finally get paid," he said.

Poor Paul. He's as clueless now as he was before, she thought. *But I guess the joke's on all of us.* Figuring it was worth a shot to stir up Paul's intuitive skills, Laura responded, "Don't you find it strange that no one has ever met Howard? I mean, how did you really meet this guy?"

"As I said before, a friend of a friend. Actually, I've been meaning to tell you this, Laura. That friend of mine actually borrowed about fifteen thousand dollars and hasn't paid me back yet. I don't think he has any intention to repay me either."

Laura immediately knew that she shouldn't have trusted Paul. She knew he meant well, but she didn't trust his ability to discern people's motives. *I guess I shouldn't have trusted myself either,* she thought as a light bulb went off in her head. *I am so judgmental. I really need to work on that. Why can I see it in everyone else but not myself?* Laura quickly remembered she was talking to Paul and replied, "So, are you going to do it … have the meeting?"

"With what money? He wants me to just conjure up three thousand dollars and plan a conference at our local Holiday Inn in a couple of weeks. I told him I couldn't do it without the money. Plus, he couldn't even tell me who was going to speak at the meeting, just that he would arrange it. I'm beginning to wonder if he keeps his word about anything. I mean, at first I thought it was just how business was done, by playing hardball. Now I don't know what to think. It almost seems like he is sabotaging the deals on purpose," Paul said.

Laura had to admit she had had that thought a couple of times as well. Paul certainly seemed to be finally waking up. She knew Paul was venting over the financial stress he must be feeling. She knew it because she was experiencing it too, only worse.

"Well, I wouldn't do it either, Paul. Good for you. I hope your friend pays you back. In the meantime, let's just continue to pray for one of these deals to close," she said.

"Absolutely," he replied.

One week later, promises of a closing of one of the Bahamas deals came by e-mail. Mike had sent a quick e-mail saying they were going to start some projects in the Bahamas that had already been approved by the prime minister. They had met with the prime minister and had been waiting all of that time for a commitment letter from his office, which they had just received. Attached to the e-mail was a copy of an official government letter with the insignia of the prime minister's office. Laura knew this was real, for she had heard the conference calls with multiple companies from the Bahamas and the prime minister's assistant on several occasions. However, she had also learned from the calls that the prime minister had requested documents from the Mildred Howard Family Trust. Deep down, Laura knew what was going to happen next, as it seemed to be a trend now. Still, she prayed for a miracle.

Back at work the following week, Laura was sitting at her desk when she had an idea. At the time, of course, she thought it was her original thought, but it was her guardian angel who was responsible. She knew that her company Health for Today, Inc., was national, so she decided to get on their website to see if there were any job openings on the East Coast to which she might be able to transfer. It was worth a shot. The CEO of Health for Today, Inc., had been more than cooperative regarding the unfortunate Packard plant debacle, and they had even become good friends after their past conversations. Laura and Ryan had wanted for some time to move out of Jupiter—*Honestly, since about a week after we moved here,* she thought—but couldn't think of a way to do it without breaking her contract.

"Good thinking, Willon," said Trylon encouragingly as he saw how Willon had given Laura her idea to move.

"That's the most brilliant idea I could have imagined. I'm so glad to have you on our team. I think Laura would be in awe if she only knew how watchful and wonderful her guardian angel was," Dunamis complimented. "Moving them out of Jupiter, as I see it, is the single best answer to this situation at this point. We have no alternatives. We need to get them into a better spiritual environment. Let's get to work on Laura's transfer before it's too late!"

Laura did an online search during lunch and found many opportunities for family physicians in the East and was especially interested in the ones in North Carolina. It was close to relatives and also had a great climate. She liked experiencing the four seasons. She called up the secretary, Paulene, saying, "Could I schedule an appointment with Mr. Taylor?"

"Sure, Dr. Carroll. He will be in town tomorrow. Will that work for you?"

"Yes, how about noon?" Laura asked.

"I'll put you down. Would you like to come here or have him come there?" Paulene asked.

"I'll come there," Laura replied.

Laura still had twenty minutes left of her lunch break and decided to text Mike. "Hey, Mike, just wondering when we might get some funds to pay our debts?"

A few minutes later, Mike responded: "Hi, Laura. It will happen when it happens. I can't make a prediction. I've got all of these owners of these companies and their lawyers and their brokers all calling me, day and night, wondering when we are going to buy their companies. Then I have my mom to worry about and her debt. And to top it off, I'm doing all of this for free. I haven't been paid one cent. You're not the only one with bills to pay."

"Thank you," she typed and put her phone away, feeling dejected.

That night, Ryan and Laura discussed her idea of transferring.

"That's a great idea, Laura. I hope Mr. Taylor agrees. I can't wait to get out of here," Ryan said.

"I can read the writing on the wall. It's obvious that things aren't going well. I don't understand it. Howard seemed so sure of himself. I wonder what went wrong."

"Well, it's also obvious that we never should have gotten involved in this mess. I mean, how stupid could we be?" Ryan stated bluntly.

"It's time for more faith. We definitely need a miracle. I don't even know where to begin. If we actually do close a deal, it doesn't even seem like there is anyone to run the companies. It seems like a big mess," Laura said.

"Let's just pray now for God's will to be done … I just remembered; we haven't been praying Psalm 91 either. I declare it over our families, our health, our finances, our property, and our pets," Ryan stated.

"Ah-h-h-men," sang Laura.

CHAPTER 24

Then he [the angel] continued, 'Do not be afraid,
Daniel. Since the first day that you set your mind to
gain understanding and to humble yourself before
your God, your words were heard, and I have come
in response to them. But the prince of the Persian
kingdom resisted me twenty-one days. Then Michael,
one of the chief princes, came to help me, because
I was detained there with the king of Persia.'
—Daniel 10:12–13

THE NEXT DAY, LAURA WENT to see Mr. Taylor.

"Hi, Paulene," she said as she walked into the office, which was next door to her office building.

"Hi, Dr. Carroll. Mr. Taylor will be right with you. I think he's just finishing up a call," she said.

"Thank you." As soon as Laura said thank you, Mr. Taylor came out from his office. "Hello, Mr. Taylor," she said.

"You can call me Patrick," he said with a smile as he beckoned her back to his office.

"Thanks, Patrick. And please call me Laura."

"Okay, Laura. What can I do for you?" he asked as he pulled out a seat at the round conference table for her.

"Well, I was thinking—things aren't going very well at my office, as you are aware, and I was wondering if maybe I could get transferred to a location owned by Health for Today, Inc., in North Carolina."

Patrick looked at her for a moment, and his eyes lit up. "You know, I love that part of the country. I've been trying to get a transfer there myself … but don't tell anyone!" he remarked. "I think that could be a possibility for you. Of course, you would have to pay back some money since you didn't live out the full contract, but I think we could negotiate that down for you."

"Sure," she said.

"But let's not get ahead of ourselves. I will talk to my supervisor to see what we can do. Do you have any specific places in mind? If you find a couple, maybe we can have you visit them," he said.

"Yes, I have a couple in mind, both close to Charlotte," she said.

"Let me work on it, and I'll be in touch," he said as he stood up and shook her hand.

"Thank you, Patrick. I really appreciate it," Laura said with a smile and walked out of the office. "Bye, Paulene. Have a nice day!"

"Bye, Dr. Carroll. You too."

Laura drove home after work, excited to tell Ryan about her conversation with Patrick.

"Hey, honey. I'm home," she said in a sing-song voice. Both of the dogs began to bark; it sounded like they were in the bedroom. She didn't hear a response from Ryan right away so she walked down the hall to the bedroom. She found Ryan lying in bed. He seemed to be just waking up.

"Hi, Ryan, How are you?" Laura asked with concern. It wasn't very often that Ryan took a nap at 5:00 p.m.

"Hi, honey," he said as he stretched out his arms over his head and yawned. "I must have fallen asleep. My stomach was starting to bother me again, so I came to lie down for a little bit."

"Oh no. How do you feel now?" Laura inquired.

"Much better. But I better not eat too much. I don't want any dinner. I'm scared that it might cause the pain to come back," Ryan said.

Laura was saddened when she heard that Ryan was having pain again. She hoped that it was just a temporary thing. Laura removed her shoes and lay down on the bed next to Ryan. They both were lying on their backs, looking at the ceiling, and Laura took Ryan's hand in hers.

"Well, on a brighter note, I spoke with Patrick Taylor today," said Laura, smiling.

"How did it go?" Ryan asked.

"Very good. I like Patrick. He's a nice guy. He said that he would try to help me find a new position. To tell you the truth, I don't think he's very happy here in Jupiter either. I guess he's only been here a year," Laura said. "I should be hearing something soon."

"Well, finally some good news," Ryan responded.

"Yeah, and now I think we should talk about our options. I don't know if I mentioned it, but Mike seemed pretty irritated with me the other day when I texted him about the deals. I have a feeling things aren't going so well. It seems so hit-or-miss. I really wish we'd get some good news. But I think we need to prepare for the worst."

"What are you thinking, Laura?" Ryan asked.

"Well, I think we should look into filing for bankruptcy. Hopefully, we won't have to, but at this point I don't even know if we can. I don't really know anything about it. At least we could see what's involved or if we could file. It beats always imagining the worst," Laura said.

"That would be fine. I don't know anything about it either. To me, it seems like such a horrible thing," Ryan said. "Never in a million years did I ever think I'd end up in the position we are in, discussing bankruptcy."

"I know. It's like a bad dream... a really bad dream," Laura said.

The next several days went by with no word from Mike about the deals or from Patrick about her possible transfer. Finally, five days after her last text to Mike, Laura got a phone call.

"Hi, Laura. How's it going?" Mike said in a cheerful tone.

"Hi, Mike. Long time, no texts," Laura responded.

"Well, I hope you are ready for some good news. I was instructed by Howard to send you some money when one of our new deals closes in a few weeks," Mike said. Laura had heard so many promises that at this point she almost let out a laugh, but she thought that it might offend Mike.

"Oh good ... what deal are you closing?" she asked, half interested.

"Well, I've been busy working with the owners of an energy company. They are coming to visit me here at my office in South Carolina next week to finalize the details. Whitney, Howard's daughter, and Chuck from Eagle Funding will be coming here also. Howard wants to purchase it and then refinance it. They will be giving us an upfront fee, of which I was told to give you ten thousand dollars. Of course, that will be until the rest of the financing comes in, which will only be ninety days," Mike finished and took a deep breath.

"Thanks for letting me know, Mike." Laura hesitated before she asked the next question. "How sure are you that we're really getting paid this time?"

"I'd say 100 percent sure, but nothing's 100 percent, so I'd say 99.999 percent sure. I mean, there is literally nothing stopping this. Everyone is on board."

After hanging up with Mike, Laura went to tell Ryan the good news. Although skeptical, Ryan hoped it was true.

"I still think we should go look into the bankruptcy," Ryan said.

"I agree. At least we'll be prepared for the worst," Laura said.

The following day, sitting at her desk in her office, Laura searched the Internet and found a bankruptcy lawyer in Dallas. She called the number and scheduled an appointment for that Friday, three days away.

She was just starting to approve prescription refills when her front office manager buzzed her on the intercom to let her know that Mr. Taylor's secretary, Paulene, was on the phone.

"Hello, Paulene," Laura said as she put the phone to her ear.

"Hi, Dr. Carroll. I have a message for you from Mr. Taylor. He wants you to know that he spoke with his supervisor, and you should expect a call from him this afternoon. His name is Bart Jenkins," Paulene said.

"Oh, great. Thank you for letting me know," Laura said.

At 4:15, Laura got a phone call on her cell phone.

"Dr. Carroll, this is Bart Jenkins. I hear good things about you from my colleague Patrick Taylor. In fact, we wouldn't even be having the conversation if it wasn't for him."

"Thank you, Mr. Jenkins, and please call me Laura."

"Please call me Bart," he responded.

"Thank you for calling, Bart."

"You're welcome. I hear you would like to be transferred. Why don't you fill me in on why?" Laura explained their situation, the misconceptions she had had about the town, and her lack of patients, as well as their desire to be closer to family on the East Coast.

After listening to her case, Bart replied, "It sounds like you need to move out of Jupiter. We can help. I'll have my assistant set up some site visits to the two locations you've chosen, and we will see what we can do about transferring you. It should be a win-win for all involved."

"Thank you so much, Bart."

"Don't thank me; thank Mr. Taylor," he replied before ending the call.

Furies was quite upset with the turn of events. He knew it was time to have a talk with Solum.

"I think it's time to change tactics," Furies said with a controlled temper.

"What do you mean?' Solum asked.

"I mean, we have to *do something else!*" he screeched, unleashing his wrath. "It's time to torment their every waking moment … and their sleep, more than before. I see now the angels are trying to help Laura and Ryan get out of Jupiter … out from under our powers. It may be too late to stop them, but we have to do what we can," Furies finished with forced decorum.

That night, Laura had a dream.

Laura and Ryan were sitting in the back row of a huge auditorium that held thousands of red velvet seats and a large balcony. There was a long stage with beautiful red velvet curtains draped across it, enclosing it like a picture in a frame. At the podium up front was a man in a tuxedo, holding an envelope. There was total silence as he opened the envelope.

"And the winner is … Dr. Laura Carroll!" the man in the tuxedo exclaimed.

All of a sudden the crowd stood to their feet and began to clap and cheer, whistle and yell. Confetti and colorful balloons started to fall to the floor. Laura stood up, surprised, and looked around. The bright spotlight had been swirling around the audience and had landed on Laura in the back row. Ryan prompted her to walk to the front.

"Go ahead, honey. Go get your award," he said with a smile.

Laura walked up on the stage and a smiling blonde woman in a long black dress came out holding a large golden trophy in the form of a dollar sign.

"Please take your trophy, Dr. Carroll," the man in the tuxedo prompted. He was still smiling, and the crowd was going ballistic. Laura took the trophy from the smiling woman and started to smile until she looked down to see what the plaque below the trophy read:

"To America's No. 1 Loser, the Most Gullible, Ridiculous Woman of the Year"

This can't be right, Laura thought and looked up at the crowd. She realized everyone was pointing and laughing at her, not cheering for her. Then she looked at the man in the tuxedo and watched as his face started to change into a grotesque-looking clown mask as he continued to cackle. His arm reached out with a long, pale, decrepit bony finger and pointed at her trophy. Laura looked down as it turned into a slimy, hissing, black coiled snake and then disintegrated into black powder. Laura started screaming in the dream and turned to run backstage. She ran through the backdoor, and the next thing she knew, she was behind a thin white curtain, sitting in a booth behind bars. She looked down and saw that she was sitting on a wooden plank with a large water basin about five feet below her. She heard a voice call through a megaphone in front of the curtain.

"Step right up! Step right up, folks, for your chance to dunk the Most Gullible Person in the World. Only fifty cents per ball, folks. Boy, is she gullible. You can't believe it until you see it. It's beyond belief folks. Just then, the curtain opened, and Laura saw a line of over one hundred people laughing and pointing at her. She was at an old-time carnival, and she was the main attraction. The people in line were holding wads of cash in their hands, and they started to fight over who would get to throw the first ball. Everyone wanted to be the first person to dunk her. Just when Laura was bracing herself for her first dunking, she looked down and saw that the water below was no longer there. In its place were hundreds of black vipers, slithering and hissing, with their eyes staring at her. As she started to scream, she heard a voice calling, "Laura, Laura."

Laura woke up, realizing it was Ryan's voice trying to wake her from a deep sleep. She opened her eyes and flinched as she saw Ryan's face. As the realization hit her that she had been dreaming, her heart rate started to decelerate.

"Are you okay, Laura? You must have been having a bad dream. You were yelling out 'no' over and over again," Ryan exclaimed.

"Yeah, I guess I was. I've never had a nightmare, but I think I just did … and I thought my real life was a nightmare," she said.

"What was it about?" Ryan asked.

"Oh, it's hard to explain … I don't even really remember most of it," Laura said, not wanting to upset Ryan.

"Let's try to go back to sleep. I think I forgot to pray Psalm 91 before bed. Let's never do that again," Ryan said. After praying, both of them fell back asleep and slept soundly for the rest of the night.

The next morning, Laura got up early. She decided to read her Bible. *What a novel idea*, she thought. Laura randomly turned to Acts 27. She started reading the story of Paul, who had been a prisoner in Caesarea. He was being transferred to Italy with some other prisoners on a ship to stand in front of Caesar. During the trip, they encountered a typhoonlike storm that left them directionless for a couple of weeks with minimal food. Finally, they came to an island called Malta. The guardian over Paul let them jump off the ship and escape so they wouldn't be killed by the prison guards. Because it was cold, as soon as he got to the island, he started to gather wood to throw on a fire. Because of the heat of the fire, a snake came out of the fire and bit Paul on the hand. Paul shook off the snake and continued about his business. The natives of Malta who were watching were waiting for Paul to drop dead from the poisonous snake, but nothing happened to him, which amazed the natives. As Laura contemplated the meaning of the story, she had an urge to turn on the television.

As she began flipping through the channels, she stopped on a station long enough to realize that the person, who turned out to be a minister, was talking about the same story in Acts 27 and 28. Knowing this wasn't a coincidence, Laura felt that God was telling her, "I didn't bring you all of this way just so you could be bitten by a snake and die."

Laura sat there for a while and thought about all the stuff that had happened to them. She realized at some point things would get better, although she didn't know when. She felt like she was learning to trust God more, rather than herself. Laura decided to say a short prayer.

"Please, God, help us," Laura prayed.

Later that day, Mike called. "Laura, I need your bank information. I'm wiring you the money tomorrow."

"Really?" she said, half stunned.

"Yep. It's a done deal," he said. Laura gave Mike her bank account information.

The following day, while Laura was at work, Mike texted her that he had wired her the money as promised. Laura checked her bank account and saw that it was there. *Finally,* she thought. *Things are turning around. It won't be long now.* Laura called Ryan to let him know. She knew they still had their appointment with the attorney the following day, although she was beginning to have second thoughts. Now, they just had to decide which bills to pay first, since it was barely enough to cover the monthly debt or what had been accumulating. Just as she was thinking about how to divide up the money, she got a phone call from Carrie, Bart's assistant.

"Hi, Dr. Carroll. I've been able to schedule your site visits for next week. You'll be able fly into Raleigh on Thursday night so you can go the clinic in Fayetteville, North Carolina, in the morning. You will spend the night and drive to Raleigh for your afternoon visit. Then you will be able to spend the night and fly out of Raleigh to come home. I'll send your itinerary by e-mail. I've also rented you a car and made hotel arrangements. How does that sound?" she asked.

"It sounds great!" Laura replied. She was truly excited to find a new position.

When she got home that night, Laura told Ryan the news. The company would only pay for one person to travel, so Ryan would have to stay home and watch the dogs. As much as she didn't like going without Ryan, she knew it would be a short trip. In all of the excitement, Laura forgot to call to cancel the meeting with the attorney.

The next day, Ryan and Laura drove to Dallas to meet with the bankruptcy attorney. Laura didn't like just not showing up and felt that it was too short notice to cancel the same morning. When they arrived, Laura saw a waiting room full of people filling out paperwork on clipboards. Ryan walked up to the window and signed in. The receptionist gave him a clipboard as well. There was a packet of information to fill out.

"Take your time, Mr. Carroll," she said.

Laura and Ryan sat down and started to fill out answers to the questions about their debt, household income, and so forth.

"We have a lot of debt to list," Laura said blankly.

After they had filled out the ten-page questionnaire, Laura and Ryan waited for their turn to go back. Neither one of them wanted to be there, but they figured it wouldn't hurt to ask some questions and tell their story to see what options they had if things didn't turn out as they expected. But

Laura was more certain than ever now that they wouldn't need to file for bankruptcy. A few minutes later, she and Ryan were called back to speak with a paralegal named Andre. When Laura and Ryan started to recount their unusual story, Andre nodded in understanding.

"You'd be surprised how common this sort of thing is. I think we have to look at all of the options. Based on your income, you may be able to file for Chapter 7. There are no guarantees, though, so you may have to go another route. Let me talk with my supervisor," he said.

While he was gone, Laura said, "I don't think we should file. Now that we finally got some money. I think we should wait to see if we get the rest of it."

"I agree. We still have a little bit of time to wait and see what happens," Ryan said.

When Andre came back into the room, he told them that they would probably be able to file for Chapter 7.

"Thank you for your time, Andre, but we're going to wait to see what happens with our situation for now. We might be in touch. We just want to wait to see," Laura said.

"Sure thing, Laura and Ryan," Andre said as he stood up and shook their hands. "I hope things turn out well for you."

Laura and Ryan walked out of the office.

"Well, it sounds better than I imagined. I had no idea how bankruptcy worked. I hope we never have to file for it," Ryan said.

"I doubt we will," Laura replied.

The following week, the first week in March, it was time for Laura's trip to North Carolina. She was excited to visit the clinics. She drove to the Dallas airport that Thursday afternoon after saying good-bye to Ryan and the pets. After an uneventful flight, Laura arrived at the airport in Raleigh, rented a car, and drove to Fayetteville. The next morning, she got up and drove to the clinic to meet with the clinic director, Barb. Laura immediately felt welcome at the clinic. It seemed to be exactly the kind of clinic where she could see herself working. All of the other employees were sweet as well. She didn't want to make up her mind, though, until she visited the clinic in Raleigh. After saying her good-byes, she went back to her hotel. She called Ryan and told him that most likely she would be choosing Fayetteville. But the question was, would they want her?

The next day, Laura drove to the clinic in Raleigh. When she walked up the steps to the clinic, a strange sense of gloom came over her. She met with the clinic director named Alan, and he gave her a tour. The employees seemed nice, but no one seemed overly friendly. After sitting down and talking about the clinic, as well as about Laura's qualifications, she thanked Alan and left. Laura felt that the Fayetteville clinic was the clinic for her. At this point, it was up to the clinic director, Barb. She hoped Barb felt the same.

A few days later, Laura received a call from Barb during her lunch break.

"Hello, Dr. Carroll," she said.

"Hi, Barb, how are you?" Laura said excitedly.

"I was calling to ask if you would like to join our staff here in Fayetteville." Barb said.

"Absolutely, Barb!" Laura replied.

"Great. How soon can you start?"

"I'll have to talk with Patrick Taylor, the CEO, and let you know," she said.

"Great. I'll wait to hear back from you. I'm excited that you're coming; we all are. I'll talk to you soon," Barb said.

"Thanks, Barb. Have a great day," Laura replied.

After the call, Laura called Ryan to tell him the good news. Then she decided to walk over to the CEO's office to see if he was available.

"Hi, Paulene, is Mr. Taylor in?" She asked.

"I believe he's in the doctors' lounge eating lunch," Paulene replied.

"I'll go check," Laura responded.

In the lounge, she found Patrick and told him the news.

"Great. Now we just have to figure out the timeline. We can discuss your contract right now if you'd like," he said.

"Sure."

"I also have some news of my own. I'll be moving next week to North Carolina myself. I'll be taking a new position," he said.

"Wow, that was quick," Laura said in surprise.

"I'll be glad to introduce you to the new interim CEO so you can discuss the contract, but we can try to agree on a payoff amount together.

I was thinking, 25 percent of the 350,000 dollars you would owe us for leaving early.

Laura quickly computed the amount in her head. "That would be around ninety thousand dollars?" Laura said.

"I think it's a little less than that, but yes," he replied.

"Well, if I don't have to pay anything on the lease for leaving early then I think that would be fine," she replied.

"Now we just have to decide on when you are going to leave."

"I was thinking in thirty days," Laura said.

"I'll see what the supervisor says," Patrick replied.

Wow, that was easy, Laura thought. What Laura didn't know was that the demons had been working overtime to get the new CEO in position before Laura's transfer. They knew he wouldn't allow the transfer. But Laura's additional prayers had been answered, and the angels had made the timing of her transfer occur prior to Patrick's leaving.

"I really appreciate all you've done to help me, Patrick," Laura said.

"No problem, Laura. It was my pleasure," he replied.

CHAPTER 25

I never saw a man who looked
With such a wistful eye
Upon that little tent of blue
Which prisoners call the sky,
And at every drifting cloud that went
With sails of silver by.
—Oscar Wilde, *The Ballad of Reading Gaol*

IT WAS MOVING DAY. IT had been thirty days since Laura's last visit with Patrick. This time around, Laura and Ryan packed their own boxes and rented a moving truck. Laura knew that Ryan would have to make a second trip to get all of the stuff they had accumulated over the years. Ryan had several "project cars," as Laura liked to call them. He really enjoyed collecting nonfunctioning and sometimes rust-covered cars and working on them in his spare time. Laura was hopeful that he would eventually finish one of them.

Ryan woke up with his stomach feeling unsettled, as he had for the past several days. He attributed it to the stress of packing up their lives yet again, renting a truck, and resettling. This was a welcomed stress to Ryan, however, no matter how chaotic it seemed.

The rental house was a small log home on a couple of acres with a functioning workshop. They were moving twenty-five minutes away from Laura's clinic, but it was the only option they could find on short notice—and one that would allow all of their pets. She hadn't been able to see it in person but had seen many photographs of it on the Internet. Laura felt that she had received confirmation about the house. When she inquired about the house by e-mail, the woman renting the house had e-mailed back. She noticed that at the bottom of her e-mail, there was a scripture from Psalm 91. She had felt her heart skip a beat when she saw it. They had been praying that Psalm over themselves every day for over a month. Ryan was also compelled to think that it was confirmation.

Laura was grateful that she didn't have to start work for thirty additional days, giving her time to unpack and explore the area. She was also happy to be closer to her mother, who would now be less than five hours away, which would allow Laura to visit her on the occasional weekend, or vice versa.

Laura would be driving separately with the pets, and Ryan and she would stop in tandem for rest stop breaks and for quick meals. The plan was to drive straight through, without having to get a hotel.

As they drove off, Laura had a sense of relief. She was excited to get out of Jupiter. She felt deep down that they were never meant to be there in the first place. As she was anticipating their new lives, her cell phone rang.

"Hi, honey," Ryan said.

"Hey, babe, what's up?" she replied.

"I'm not feeling very well. I think I'm going to have to stop for a while at the next rest stop we see. I want you to go on without me since you have all of the pets," he said.

"Are you sure, Ryan?" she asked.

"Yep, I'll be fine," he said, but Laura was unconvinced. She had seen him when the stomach pain was at its worst.

"I'll start praying for you. We can meet at the next stop, and then I'll go on," Laura said.

"Okay," Ryan replied.

After they stopped at the rest stop, Laura drove on to Fayetteville and periodically checked in with Ryan. She breathed a sigh of relief after she was able to get to the house and found the keys waiting for her under the front door mat. She went into the home, and her first thought was that it seemed pretty small, but she wasn't going to complain. The kitchen was small but had been updated with granite countertops and a gas cooktop with six burners. For Laura, that was her favorite thing about the house. She could cook all day in a kitchen like that. *What's wrong with having to keep some things packed up in the attic?* she thought as she continued to look around at the small living area and bedrooms.

When Ryan eventually pulled into the driveway two hours later, Laura was relieved. She went out to greet him. He was still having pain and hadn't eaten anything all day. It was a struggle unpacking the truck, but they took out what they would need for the night and left everything else for the morning.

In the morning, Ryan was feeling slightly better, and they unpacked the truck so they could return it to the nearby truck rental company.

Neither Laura nor Ryan had told Mike, Howard, or anyone else from that venture that they were moving. They didn't feel it was necessary at that point. Laura had texted Howard on several occasions and had not heard anything from him. Mike would send over e-mails periodically about the deal they had with the energy company, but Laura had no idea what was happening, and Mike didn't respond to her texts either. It seemed like after she received the ten thousand dollars, everything went quiet.

A few weeks went by, and Laura and Ryan got settled into their new home. They were both happy to be in North Carolina, but they were getting concerned about not hearing much from Mike.

In the heavenly realm, Dunamis was growing concerned as well.

"I think we may have a problem," Dunamis said to Arnamis and some of his lieutenants sitting in his office.

"What do you mean?" Arnamis replied. He was under the impression that once Laura and Ryan moved from Jupiter, all would be well.

"Well, I see that there is a large presence of demonic spirits trying to break into the highly guarded region of Fayetteville, North Carolina, to where Ryan and Laura have moved. Unfortunately, I believe they are making some headway," he replied.

"Aren't they out of harm's way now?" Arnamis replied.

"Well, technically they are, but we still have some unfinished business to address. This current problem they are having is coming to an end, but I don't know how Laura and Ryan will handle it," Dunamis said with concern. "I have hope that they will be able to endure the outcome, but I'm not sure how they will handle the time leading up to it. Let's not get complacent. We still have a lot of work to do."

It was April 21 at 6:30 p.m., a day and time that Laura would never forget. It was similar to the day she was notified of Stan Powers's death.

She replayed that event over and over in her mind like the scene of a movie. And every time she replayed it, the images were as clear in her mind as if it had just happened. And there was no way to delete it.

Laura's cell phone rang as they finished eating dinner. She knew it was Mike because his name came up on her phone screen as it rang.

"Hi, Laura. This is Mike," he said.

"Oh, hi, Mike. How are you?" she asked, as if she had just talked to him yesterday.

"Well, I've got some news for you. Are you sitting down?" he asked.

Really? she thought. *Why do people always have to be sitting down to hear bad news?* She assumed it was bad news by his tone of voice.

"Yep," Laura said succinctly, even though she wasn't. She just wanted him to get to the point. She had felt a sense of anger spring up in her with his question. She began to resent him thoroughly. She had recently concluded that he and his "updates" had had control over her for too long. And the last thing she wanted to do now was listen to his instruction about sitting down. Laura had felt that things weren't going well for a long time, and now—just maybe—Mike was going to admit it, both to himself and to her.

Mike started to speak in his usual suspenseful manner, consciously controlling his audience by making her cling to every word. She had walked into the bedroom to get away from the loud clanging of pots and pans in the kitchen as Ryan washed the dishes.

"I was checking the mail yesterday after my ten-mile run," Mike said, "and I got a letter from Howard. It was a handwritten letter, which I thought was interesting."

Get to the point, Laura thought.

"Anyway, if you have ever wondered why we haven't been able to find out where Howard lives, it's because his home is the Mississippi State Penitentiary in Parchman, Mississippi. And his real name is Gary Christopher Scott."

Wow, Laura thought as a lot of things started to come together in her mind and make sense. She walked into the kitchen and made motions to Ryan, who had a perplexed look on his face as he tried to figure out if what Laura was hearing on the other end of the phone was good news or bad news.

"When did you find out?" Laura said.

"About a week ago. I was trying to figure out the best way to let you know. I'll be calling Paul next," Mike finished.

"So, *how* did *you* find out?" she asked.

"Well, I received a letter, like I said, and his return address was the penitentiary. I guess he decided to finally come clean. He had been in solitary confinement and wasn't able to have a cell phone so he had to send instructions by writing. He apparently had no choice," Mike surmised.

"I didn't think inmates were allowed cell phones," Laura said, still thinking about all of the things that had occurred and the reason why Howard, or "Gary Scott," would never call back when he said he would or had to call late at night.

"They aren't. I guess Whitney always sneaked one in for him," Mike said.

"What about the Skype thing?" she asked.

"I guess they found a way to do that too," Mike said.

Laura thought about the "stroke" he'd had and the car accident, as well as the "poor health" that prevented him from traveling. Finally, she asked, "What's he in prison for?"

This question caused Ryan to give Laura a questioning glance.

"Well, I Googled him, and I think I found him. He is serving a life sentence for cocaine smuggling and creating shell companies. I think he's originally from Saint Lucia. Now his daughter Whitney tells me that she had been wanting to tell me the truth for a long time but just couldn't do it because she didn't know how I'd react," Mike said.

"Who knew? Did Adam know?" Laura asked.

"Yes, he knew. I guess he assumed it was okay," Mike said.

"So lying to us about Howard's—I mean, Gary's—identity is okay? As if we would have agreed to be credit partners with a known felon?" Laura said. Now Ryan was catching on and was listening to every word Mike said—Laura had put him on speaker phone.

"Yeah, I guess it's not illegal to do business with someone in prison," Mike said.

"Really? Well, it's definitely a scam to get people involved unknowingly," Laura said. She decided to try to Google him herself. While she was doing her own Internet search, Mike said he had to call Paul.

"So, Mike, before you go … are you going to report this? I mean, what do we do… call the FBI?" Laura asked.

"When I first found out I called the FBI, and no one really seemed that interested in what happened," Mike said.

"Maybe they just didn't understand … seems strange," Laura said.

"Yeah, well, I'll be talking with a lawyer to see what I should do. I mean, I don't have any money to hire one, though."

"Well, let me know what you decide to do. I'll talk to you later."

When Laura got off of the phone, she told Ryan the whole conversation.

"Wow, everything is starting to make sense now … but how was he able to be on the phone like that all of the time? It doesn't make sense," Ryan said.

"I know. Let's see what we can find about Gary online."

After searching for only a few minutes, Laura was able to find a newspaper article about Gary's conviction. He was a cocaine dealer and smuggler who made different shell companies to hide his endeavors. He was also known as "the Monster" because he tried to put contracts out on witnesses to have them killed. Laura started to be concerned for her own safety at that point. She was glad that they hadn't let anyone know they were moving and decided to keep it to themselves.

The moment Laura got the call from Mike, she knew the entire ordeal that they had been going through was over. She knew that she would never have to speak to any of them ever again if she chose not to, and at that moment, both Ryan and Laura chose not to. That was the simplest decision of all.

Laura and Ryan had to decide what to do next. They realized that the first thing they needed to do was try to file bankruptcy, if possible. Even though they were now in North Carolina, Laura decided to call the bankruptcy lawyer in Dallas. It was two hours earlier there, and she was hoping she could still reach someone at the office. She quickly found the number and dialed it. She was relieved when someone answered.

"Hi, this is Laura Carroll. I want to speak with Andre, the paralegal, if he's still in," Laura said.

"He just left, but his supervisor is still here. Would you like to speak with him? His name is John Morgan," the receptionist said.

"Sure."

When the attorney, John Morgan, got on the line, Laura explained the situation to him as best as she could. Even as the words came out of her mouth, it sounded surreal. She could only imagine what John was thinking.

"Well, Dr. Carroll, I think a couple of things. You have to cover yourself. I mean, someone may think that you and your husband were in this from the beginning. If I were you, I'd probably not do anything. Just not pay any of the debt back and hope no one sues you. And if they do sue you, then you could just hire a lawyer. But I don't think this is a case we can help you with," John said.

That was not what Laura wanted to hear. The advice seemed horrible. *How could anyone in their right mind think that we would have been involved in this from the beginning?* Laura thought.

"Thanks, Mr. Morgan," Laura said. She knew there was no use trying to convince this guy of anything. They had so much material and so many documents that they wouldn't have any trouble with people believing that they had absolutely *not* known Howard's, or Gary's, real identity. Laura had been saying Howard's name for so long, she was having trouble thinking of him in any other way.

"No problem," he replied and hung up.

Laura started to grow concerned, though. She told Ryan what Mr. Morgan had said. It was obvious that they needed another opinion. *A second opinion for the doctor,* Laura thought. It was too late in the evening to call anyone else, so Laura did a search for some lawyers in the local area and wrote down some phone numbers to call in the morning. That night, Laura tossed and turned. She was being emotionally tormented by Solum in her sleep. For the demons, this was Laura and Ryan's weakest point yet, and it was the perfect time to strike.

Laura was sleeping in her new home in North Carolina. She heard a strange noise that woke her up. Laura pinched herself and thought she was awake. She was convinced of it. The dogs were still asleep, so Laura thought she was just imagining the noise. *I better go back to sleep,* she thought.

Then, Ryan said in the dark, "I think we better buy some guns. Gary Christopher Scott may send someone to kill us."

Laura's greatest fears were being realized. What had happened to them? Why were their lives so rotten? So horrible? *God, why did you let this happen to us? I mean, how can it get any worse?* Laura began to cry in the dark in her sleep. *How broken do I have to be?*

And in her dream, God interrupted and spoke to her a simple truth: "Completely, Laura. You have to be completely broken. That's the only way I can build you back up to be the person you are meant to be."

Laura woke up in the night. She realized everything had been a dream: the noise, Ryan talking about Gary Scott sending a killer, and God speaking to her. But deep down she knew God had spoken to her. She realized she hadn't listened to God the way she should have. *Maybe talking to me in my sleep was the only way I would listen,* she thought.

The demon Solum was not expecting the presence of God in Laura's bedroom. He had the unfortunate realization of his powerlessness in the situation and shrank back into the corner of Laura's room as the glory of God filled it. In the demonic realm, Solum began to tremble as he watched his very own flesh begin to melt off his bones, and he disintegrated into a decayed corpse on Ryan and Laura's floor. Tat and Furies retrieved the spiritual decaying mass of Solum and brought it back to their base in order to revive him. But Solum was forever to be a shrunken shadow of himself; although still able to feel pain and torment, he was less than alive but not quite dead.

When Furies reported the news to Wink, he reacted as expected.

"Solum was stupid enough to not prepare for this sort of thing. It serves him right. I suppose that you are now too scared to continue with the battle at hand," Wink said with intimidation.

"Oh, no. We are prepared to engage. But I may have to rethink my strategy," Furies said, while trying to maintain his composure. He was rattled and clueless as to what to do next.

"Good. Try not to get yourself destroyed like your colleague here," he said as he pointed to Solum, who was now just a pile of nondescript black goo that Wink had placed with a spatula on a small metal tray. "I think I will place him on the shelf in my study as a reminder of what happens when we let our guard down!" Wink snarled.

Furies began to think of all of the things that had happened and now, here he was, looking at his fallen comrade, Solum. Solum had been so sure of himself, so wise. It was obvious there was a lot to learn from this experience, and Furies wasn't sure if he was ready to continue in his current state of mind. However, he didn't want Wink to know.

"Tat and I will reconvene and go over some new strategies to employ, Wink. We won't let you down," Furies said. In the back of his mind, he was thinking of how easily Solum had been destroyed. *It was almost too easy,* he thought. *Perhaps he was deceived about the size of the threat.*

"If you do, you'll regret it," Wink threatened as he watched Furies slink out of sight.

Unaware of the battle raging around them and their victory from the previous night, Laura and Ryan continued to think about Gary Christopher Scott.

"I think all of his daughters should be arrested," Laura said.

"I know. Look what he is teaching them. It's horrible. We can't even tell anyone about this; it's too embarrassing," Ryan said.

"I know. Mike texted me last night, that Gary's stupid daughter is still trying to get him to close a deal with yet another company and just not tell the people what they are really going to do with the money they are getting from them. It's making me angry. I have to say, though, that after thinking about it, you would think his being in prison would kind of help to prove how unlikely it is that we could have been involved as knowing, willing partners in crime, wouldn't it?" Laura asked. She was worried that no one would believe they had been the unknowing victims of Gary Scott.

"Yeah, any person who knows us would realize that," Ryan said.

"I guess I'll call another lawyer this morning. There has to be somebody out there who can help us," Laura said.

CHAPTER 26

And the God of all grace, who called you
to his eternal glory in Christ, after you have
suffered a little while, will himself restore you
and make you strong, firm and steadfast.
—1 Peter 5:10

LAURA PICKED UP HER CELL phone and called the 800 number of the first lawyer's office on her list of bankruptcy specialists—Sabon, Sterling, and Klein. Their office was located in Fayetteville.

On the third ring, a male voice answered. "Sterling here."

"Hello, Mr. Sterling. I didn't think I'd get a lawyer right away," Laura said.

"Yep, it's my turn for phone duty," he said, chuckling.

"Well, I was hoping I could get some advice about a possible bankruptcy my husband and I might file, but it's a little more complicated than that," Laura said.

"I specialize in complicated. Fire away."

Laura explained her situation the best she could and then drew her narrative to a close.

"If everything you say is true and happened the way you said it did, I think you should be able to file for bankruptcy. It sounds like you were the victim of emotional terrorism. That's what I call it. Let me talk to my colleagues about it, and we can talk tomorrow around the same time. Would that be okay?" He asked.

"Sure," Laura said with a sigh of relief. She was delighted to hear him speak those words.

"Have a nice day, Laura."

"You too."

The next day Laura called back to speak with Mr. Sterling. The phone rang several times before the answering machine turned on. Laura tried to call several more times and left a couple of messages over the following two days but got no response. She was perplexed. He had seemed so helpful and nice, and she didn't understand why he didn't return her calls. *It must be a lawyer thing*, she thought. She decided to call another lawyer's office on her list. The second name on the list was Alexa, Barron, and Carpenter. Their office was also conveniently located in Fayetteville. It looked like they also had an office in Raleigh, which seemed like a good thing to Laura. Laura made another phone call.

The receptionist was quick to answer.

"Hello, I'd like to talk with someone about filing for bankruptcy," she stated quietly.

After a short amount of time, the receptionist said,

"Ms. Sarah Carpenter is available today at five o'clock."

"That would be great," Laura said.

"She will be at the Fayetteville location," the receptionist added.

"Even better," said Laura.

At five that evening, Laura and Ryan showed up at the office of Ms. Sarah Carpenter. It was in an older Victorian-style home in a quiet part of town, away from other businesses.

"This is a quaint office," Laura said as they walked up the creaking wooden steps of the older home onto the porch with peeling paint. There was a handwritten sign in the front window that read, "Please knock loudly". Ryan knocked on the door, and the receptionist answered.

"Hello, you must be the Carrolls," she said.

"Yes," they said in response.

"Great, have a seat. I have a few papers for you to fill out, and she will be right with you. By the way, my name is Kelley, if you need anything."

"Thank you," Laura said. Laura and Ryan answered the questions on the paperwork, which was similar to the paperwork supplied by the Dallas firm. Laura had brought that along with her just in case.

After a few minutes, they heard footsteps coming down the winding wooden stairway. A female in her thirties approached them. She was wearing a gray dress, and Laura's first impression was that she looked like Jodie Foster.

"Hello, I'm Sarah Carpenter. You must be the Carrolls."

"Yes, hello. Thank you for meeting with us today. My name is Laura, and this is my husband, Ryan," Laura said shaking her hand. *She even sounds like Jodie Foster,* Laura thought, amused.

"Let's go into this conference room here, and you can let me know what's going on," Sarah said as she walked into a room with a long mahogany table and several wooden chairs on either side. They all sat together at one end of the table, and Laura began recounting the last couple of years, focusing on the last year in particular, as it related to "Howard Holland". Sarah interrupted only briefly to ask questions of clarification.

At the end of the summary, Sarah said, "It sounds like a movie."

"Yeah, we know," Ryan and Laura said in unison.

"I guess truth can be stranger than fiction," Laura said, knowing how unique and somewhat unbelievable their situation truly was.

After asking a few other questions about the debt and reviewing Laura's old paperwork from the Dallas firm, Sarah said, "You came to the right place. We can help you. Have you reported anything to anyone?"

"No, we didn't know what to do," Ryan replied.

"I'll have to talk to my colleague. He will probably suggest reporting this to the US Attorney's Office. And they may or may not want to talk to you. They might just ignore it. It's hard to predict. But it would obviously look better for you to go to them first so they don't think you are trying to hide something. Also, it would be good if you could give me e-mails, paperwork, or anything else you might think is relevant to this so we can display full disclosure," Sarah said.

Ryan and Laura both exhaled.

"That's great. We'll give you everything we have," Laura said. "I'll just start printing off all of my e-mails. There are so many, though, I may have to just give you a little bit of everything, so you can see all of the deals that Howard Holland—that is, Gary Christopher Scott—was trying to do," Laura said.

"That's fine. You can just drop them off, and we can make copies as needed," Sarah replied. "Again, don't worry. We can help."

"Great. I'll drop off the papers tomorrow evening," Laura said.

As they were leaving, Laura said to Ryan, "I was really concerned, but Sarah made me feel so much better."

"Yeah, me too. I can't wait to get this all behind us," Ryan replied.

In the demonic realm, Tat and Furies had a very private conversation.

"I'm convinced that Wink knew the danger he was putting Solum in," Furies whispered.

"Yeah, I'm starting to be suspicious of Wink myself," Tat responded, trying to take the focus for any wrongdoing off himself. He was very willing to throw Wink under the bus in light of their failed mission.

"Maybe we should reassess our mission and redirect our focus to taking Wink out before we continue our battle against Ryan and Laura," Furies suggested. Furies knew that it was a dangerous idea at its onset, but he believed in the long run, it would be the only way to ensure his survival and ultimate promotion. *And there is strength in numbers, after all,* he thought. The more demons they could bring on board to undermine Wink, the better their chances of success.

The demons didn't know that there was an unseen presence nearby them, listening to every word of their "private" discussion. Dunamis had been very pleased to see that the demons were about to undergo a huge power struggle internally—which meant for the time being, they had won the battle, and the demons had retreated. He could only cheer on the lower demons as they did his work for him.

In the following weeks, Sarah filed for Chapter 7 bankruptcy on behalf of Laura and Ryan and reported their situation to the US Attorney's Office. Laura started her new job at the clinic. She felt that, at least for the moment, that was right where God wanted her to be. And Laura learned to want to be exactly where God wanted her to be. Ryan started working on a new project car and began the process of starting his tree service again. Laura had been instructed by Sarah not to talk to anyone who had been involved in the deals with Gary Christopher Scott, which was fine with her. Mike had tried to text a few times, but Laura just ignored him. It felt good to be free from the grips of the madman Howard Holland and his cohorts. She didn't think Mike had known about "Howard," but she couldn't know for sure, and she knew, deep down, it really didn't matter. She just wanted this to be behind her.

Two months later, the phone rang. It was Sarah.

"Guess what, Laura? You got your discharge. No more debt," she said excitedly.

"Great news!" Laura said. She put her mouth over the phone and told Ryan the good news. She still wondered, though, if the US Attorney's Office would be in touch. She hadn't heard anything from anyone. As much as she wanted to stop Gary Christopher Scott and his daughters, she didn't like the idea of having to talk with the US Attorney.

"Congratulations to you both. I know this has been hard for you guys. Take care," Sarah said.

"Thanks, Sarah," Laura replied. After she hung up the phone, she turned to Ryan and said, "Why do you think this happened to us?"

"I don't know. It's obvious we had a lot to learn, and God has a great way of giving us a tailor-made lesson in light of all of our mistakes," he said.

"But I don't really understand. I guess when I look back, we had many—I mean, *many*—red flags, but we ignored them all. I guess maybe God had been trying to talk to us through people as well. And here we were, thinking we knew better than God. He must be amused by us humans sometimes," she said.

"Well, God did not cause this to happen, but he will use what is meant for our harm and turn it into a blessing," Ryan said.

"What do you think the blessing is in all of this mess?" Laura asked.

"Well, it's obvious we have grown closer to God. I think God wants to show us the direction we need to go, and we should realize we will always fail if we try to live our own lives without him," Ryan said.

"Yeah, there are so many people out there like us. Maybe our story can help some of them avoid the anguish we went through. I almost feel embarrassed, though, to talk about it. I mean, I think of all of the people who might judge us," Laura said.

"We have to be more concerned about what God thinks, rather than what people think, Laura," Ryan said.

"I know you're right, Ryan. I don't know about you, but I'm ready to start over—this time, the right way, with God in control," Laura said.

"Yes, me too. It's a new beginning," Ryan said as they hugged.

ABOUT THE AUTHOR

JILL VAN HORN IS A family physician who lives with her husband and son near Greensboro, North Carolina. She enjoys reading and has decided to put her hand to writing a book as a new author. She bases her first book on a circumstance from her past that taught her and her husband about one characteristic of human nature that can cause the most well-meaning individuals to overlook good judgement and put their trust in individuals rather than God. Or can cause certain individuals to perpetrate acts towards fellow humans that lead to destruction. That characteristic is greed. She is writing this book as a warning to all about the seemingly increasing number of financial schemes that have been occurring in the present day. Her hope is to bring awareness to the fraudulent "wolves in sheep's clothing" that try to take advantage of the unsuspecting "sheep".

Printed in the United States
By Bookmasters